WESTWARD BOUND
✿ *A* GATES *Family Mystery* ✿

By Catherine H

Based on characters created

motion picture "National Treasure"

Screenplay by Jim Kouf and Cormac Wibberley & Marianne Wibberley

Story by Jim Kouf and Oren Aviv & Charles Segars

And characters created for the theatrical motion picture

"National Treasure: Book of Secrets"

Screenplay by The Wibberleys

Story by Gregory Poirier and The Wibberleys & Ted Elliott & Terry Rossio

𝕯𝖎𝖘𝖓𝖊𝖞 PRESS
New York

Thank you to those who started this hunt:
Oren Aviv, Charles Segars, and Jim Kouf

Special thanks to Jerry Bruckheimer
and Jon Turteltaub

WESTWARD BOUND

A GATES *Family Mystery*

June 1848
Carrollton Manor,
near Annapolis, MD

James Monroe Gates stood by the window in the parlor of his family's home, feeling a bit uncomfortable in the midst of the raucous gaiety that was currently filling the modest house. His elder sister, Eleanor, married to Arthur nearly thirty minutes now, was presiding over the levee following her wedding ceremony, to which their father seemed to have invited all and sundry. James spotted one neighbor partaking eagerly of the wedding refreshments along with his wife and five grown sons. Across the room, another set of neighbors were cavorting with several people James had never set eyes on before. Taking it all in, he couldn't help but wonder how much of the family's meager income his father had spent on this party.

"Some frolic, eh?" A voice cut into his thoughts. James turned to see the groom's younger brother, David, standing there grinning at him. His round cheeks were showing spots of red from the heat of the room and, perhaps, from the liquid refreshments as well. "Most every soul in Maryland must be here."

"True enough." James glanced around the crowded room. "Though I don't see why Father had to invite so many people."

"You can't blame the old man for going the whole hog." David shrugged. "He isn't growing any younger, eh? And El's his only daughter, after all."

That was true enough. In addition to being the only girl in a family of males, Eleanor was named after her father's beloved twin sister, who had moved to far-off California nearly fifteen years earlier with her explorer husband. Perhaps it should be no wonder that Adam Benjamin Gates, at a remarkably well-preserved sixty-two years of age, wished to make this occasion special for the younger Eleanor. He had even managed to procure for her the white satin dress of her dreams, modeled closely after that worn by Queen Victoria of England some eight years ago. James had to admit that in it, Eleanor, normally a rather sour and argumentative person, had never looked so lovely nor so happy.

"Still, Father might think a bit more of the future," he mused, now speaking more to himself than to David. "We can ill afford to spend all our money on one day, whatever the circumstance."

David appeared unconcerned. "No need for worry," he said. "Arthur has a mind to make something great of your family's hack business. It won't be long till he's set things back on track, I'll warrant. And none too soon," he added with a glance at the room's well-worn furnishings.

James clenched his fists at his sides. So his new brother-in-law planned to "make something great of" the family business, did he? He wasn't sure he liked that prospect. It was bad enough that he had spent his whole life being ruled by his three older brothers—intelligent but mercurial Thomas; rough, careless Will; and self-assured Sam. Was he now to be the servant of his sister's high-handed, self-important, and generally rather insufferable new husband, Arthur, as well?

As David moseyed off, James found himself brooding over his life. For as long as he could remember, he'd felt a strong hankering to be his own man, in charge of his own destiny for once rather than a victim of his family's somewhat poor circumstances. Now that he was eighteen, he had hoped finally to achieve this goal. But somehow, it seemed farther from his grasp than ever.

Such thoughts scattered as he saw his father approaching. "There you are, son," Adam Gates said, his eyes wandering past his youngest son's face to a point somewhere over his left shoulder. He seemed to be chewing something over in his mind. "Need to tell you something before I forget."

"What is it?" James asked warily, sure that he would not like whatever it was his father had to say. The two had never been completely at ease with each other. His brother Will, who never hesitated to voice any thought that entered his mind, had often said it was because their mother had died giving birth to James, and Adam had never forgiven it.

For his part, James thought the blame could be placed on Adam. He couldn't help but wonder what had possessed his father to uproot the entire family upon the death of his own father, moving abruptly from Concord, Massachusetts, to Maryland mere weeks before James was born. Had that journey weakened his mother just enough to take her from this life at the moment of his arrival in it? He would never know, but his active mind constantly imagined what life might be like had the move never happened. Would his mother still be alive to this day? Would James have found the acceptance, care, and companionship among his Concord cousins that he had always felt he lacked with his father and brothers? Would their branch of the family now be prosperous and respected, rather than the laughingstock of the neighborhood?

He grimaced slightly, glancing around the crowded room and wondering which of their neighbors might be whispering behind their hands about the Gates family even now, while drinking their apple brandy and eating their food. As James looked about, his gaze fell upon his brother Thomas, who was nearby, deep in an intense discussion with another young man.

That was no surprise, as everything about Thomas Gates could be described as intense. James's earliest memories of his eldest brother were of a fresh-faced, ginger-haired, smiling youth who always enjoyed entertaining him with games and riddles. But that Thomas had matured into the current one, one who barely acknowledged James's existence anymore—or anything else aside from a certain slip of paper containing just five words: *The secret lies with Charlotte.*

It had begun when James was a toddler. Back then, Adam and his two eldest boys had been in the employ of Charles Carroll of Carrollton. Adam had been the stable manager and his sons stableboys. One rainy night in 1832, the teenage Thomas had been called out of bed to drive an ailing Mr. Carroll to Washington to see then-President Andrew Jackson. James was a bit uncertain of the details, but some-how the old man had passed to Thomas that mysterious slip of paper, which both Thomas and Adam seemed convinced was the clue to some immense, hidden treasure.

Carroll had died soon after, and his estate, Carrollton Manor, had been divided up among his heirs. Adam had struck out on his own on a tiny share of the land, building a small hack business consisting of a couple of coaches and a half dozen horses. Thanks to his good eye for horseflesh, the business had started off well. But since those early days, Adam had spent less and less time working to support his family and more and more time trying to decipher the "Charlotte" clue along with Thomas.

James had not heard most of this family history from his father or Thomas, of course—neither of them bothered to talk to him much. But Will was old enough to remember most of it, and had filled him in over the years.

In any case, the "Charlotte" clue was only one part of what James saw as the entire family's overall humiliation. For as long as he could remember, his father and Thomas had shared an interest—some would say obsession—with treasure hunting. During their infrequent visits to Maryland, James's cousin told him that this was some sort of family trait passed down from the earliest Gates men to arrive in the New World two centuries earlier. Even some of the Concord cousins spent their leisure time searching out bits of lost jewelry and such. However, James doubted that anyone else in the family had made such fools of themselves as had his father and older brother. Thomas had yet to show any interest in taking a wife, and Adam left most of the day-to-day work of the stable to his two younger sons.

It had not gone unnoticed by their small community. Years of seeing other people whisper and laugh whenever a Gates went by had left James with an intense distaste for anything having to do with treasure. He was destined for something different. In fact his goal was to strike out on his own as soon as he was able—work hard, create his own life, and earn enough wealth—*real* wealth, not imaginary treasure—to buy himself some respect and banish the looks and titters once and for all.

Until then, however, he was stuck. "I'll need you to travel with Thomas to Washington city week after next," Adam said now, jolting James out of his reverie. "You've heard about the cholera epidemic in New York?"

"Of course." James tried not to grimace at the thought of being stuck in a coach with Thomas all the way to Washington and back. "What of it?"

"Franklin Poole lives in New York City." Adam rubbed his chin and smiled, a faraway look coming into his eyes. "He wants to send his son Seamus to us for a while to keep him safe from the disease."

"Oh." James had heard his father mention the Pooles often. Franklin had been somehow involved in the great exploits Adam and his twin sister, Eleanor, had shared when they were around James's age. This had sparked a lifelong friendship with the Gates family, though James was fuzzy on any details beyond that. Not for the first time, he was tempted to ask his father to tell him more about those days. But as always, he held his tongue.

"Your cousin Duncan is coming down from Concord

for business in Washington this Independence Day," Adam went on, his attention already wandering back to Eleanor, who was hanging upon her new husband's arm nearby. "Thomas has offered to meet him there if he will pick up Seamus Poole along the way. That way Duncan will not have to make a detour to deliver him here—he is very busy, you see." He tipped his head as if in deference to the more successful branch of the family tree.

"And can Thomas not manage it on his own?" James asked, honestly perplexed.

His father blinked at him, as if confused by the question. "There is to be a celebration that day—they are laying the cornerstone for the new monument to the late President Washington," he said. "Thomas has some interest in attending, and wishes not to keep track of young Poole during the festivities."

James bit back a quick response. What use was it to point out that he was being asked to waste a full day on a task his older brother could easily handle himself should he only be willing to put a mind to it? What Thomas wanted, Thomas got—at least as far as their father was concerned.

"Besides," Adam said quickly, clearly noting his son's

displeased expression, "you are closest of any of us to young Seamus's age. Surely it is best that you are there to greet him and make him feel at home."

James nodded, forcing a smile. He had no intention of spoiling this happy day by arguing with his father. However, he couldn't help but guess that his age was not the primary reason he was being sent on this errand. It was more likely that he was the family member his father considered best spared to satisfy Thomas's whim. Even though he was twice the horseman Will was and far better with customers than Sam, he found himself always shunted aside, ignored, forgotten. . . .

Feeling out of sorts, he waited until his father wandered off and then turned toward the back of the house, seeking a moment of quiet. The door to his father's tiny study was shut, and James reached for it. However, when he entered, he immediately spotted a pair of neighbors bent over his father's cluttered desk.

"Oh!" One of the trespassers, a stout man named Miller, looked up quickly. "Er, hello there, son. We was just, er . . ."

The second man was a stranger to James. "We was just curious, that's all," he said. "Didn't mean no harm." With a soothing smile, he scuttled from the room with Miller close behind him.

James glared after the two men, a mixture of irritation and shame rooting him to the spot for a moment. Was his father such a spectacle that even his own neighbors found no shame in rooting through his belongings? Sighing, James turned to tidy the desk where the pair had been digging around.

While doing so, a stack of about a dozen loosely tied letters caught his eye. The writing was loopy and bold, and upon closer examination he saw that the return address read Ellie Gates Darby, California Territory.

He blinked. The letters were from his Aunt Eleanor! He'd never heard any mention of news from her, whereas other relatives' letters were read aloud at the supper table. Had his father kept these letters a secret from the family— or only failed, as usual, to mention it to *him*?

James stared at the packet of letters a moment, his curiosity stirred. His father talked so little of his adventures out West, or even of his sister. Perhaps glancing through these letters would help him understand the old man better, discover what secrets he'd always withheld. . . .

A muffled shout of laughter erupted in the other room, startling James. On impulse, he quickly grabbed the letters and tucked them into his clothes. Vowing to return them to the desk before his father noticed their absence, he hurried out to rejoin the party.

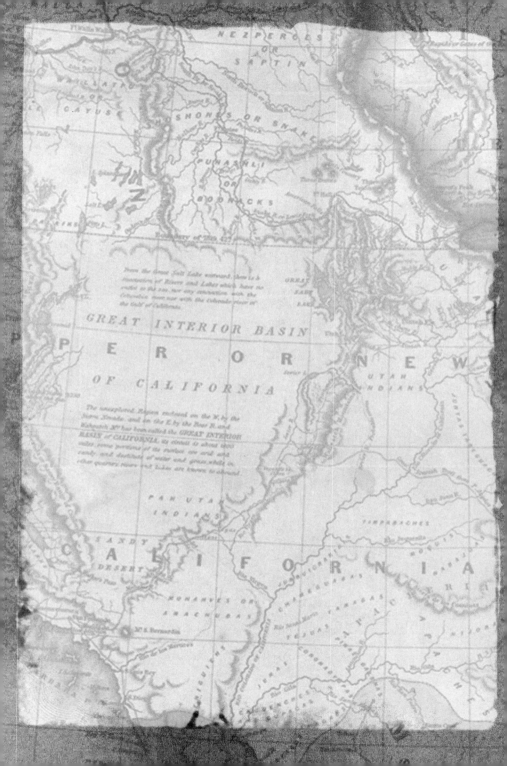

One

"Thomas will be along after a spell. He wanted to hear some of the speeches." James forced a rather uncomfortable smile. His cousin Duncan had just departed, leaving him feeling ill at ease and uncertain what to say next as he stood with the slight, dark-haired, vulpine-faced stranger, Seamus Poole.

"No hurry on my account," Seamus said, seeming untroubled by the awkwardness of the occasion—and in fact acting as though he and James had been acquainted all their lives. "I don't mind having a look about Washington city myself. It's where my father lived when he first came to this country from Ireland, did you know? And, of course, it's especially interesting on a day such as this—as these carryings-on are all being brought to us by the fraternal order of Freemasons." He waved one skinny hand at the crowds surrounding them. "Your Cousin Duncan's paying passenger today was himself a Mason, in fact, but Dunc wouldn't allow me to mention it the entire trip down here, the bootlicker! So I shall have to settle for observing the Masons on my own and seeing what I can see." Seamus finally stopped speaking to catch his breath.

James glanced around, too distracted by all the activity to follow much of what Seamus was talking about. On that particular July Fourth, the capital city was alive with more people than he'd ever seen in one place before—thousands of them, perhaps tens of thousands. Even though his father had told him there would be a celebration in honor of the late President Washington that day, James had not been expecting anything like this.

An enormous arch had been set up at the site of the future monument, with brightly colored ribbons of red, white, and blue fluttering in the light summer breeze. The sun shone brightly down upon the immense white marble cornerstone that was the first part of the monument to be completed as well as the awnings shading the temporary seating. Throngs of excited citizens crowded into the seats and surrounding areas, trying to get close enough to hear the orators. President Polk himself was seated on the podium, along with various other dignitaries. A marching band and a number of fire companies were at hand, all of them colorfully dressed in their best uniforms. At the moment, a man in his late thirties was delivering a lengthy, but stirring, speech.

"Who is that, I wonder?" James commented.

A smooth-faced, towheaded boy around his own age was standing just in front of them and turned to answer. "That would be Mr. Winthrop," the stranger said in a rich, clear voice. "He is the current Speaker of the House of Representatives."

James tilted his head in thanks to the stranger, feeling a bit sheepish for not recognizing the rather famous man. Meanwhile, Seamus tugged at his sleeve.

"Come, let's try to get closer," he urged. "I wish to get a better view of the big bugs on the platform. All creation appears to be up there! I wonder how many of them are Freemasons?"

James hesitated only momentarily, glancing around for any sign of Thomas. But his brother had disappeared into the crowd well before Duncan's appointed arrival time, little concerned with whether Seamus made it safely to Washington or not. He wasn't likely to be looking for either of them anytime soon.

As he and Seamus wandered deeper into the crowd, James found that he had little need to work at keeping the conversation going. Seamus barely seemed to pause for breath as he chattered merrily, leaping from one topic to the next like a squirrel leaping from branch to branch, leaving James a bit dizzy as he tried to follow along.

Despite his father's optimistic prediction that the two of them would have much in common due to their closeness in age, it soon became clear to James that this was not the case. Not only were they near opposites in physical appearance— Seamus being short and wiry while James was tall and sturdily built; the visitor's hair being as dark and wild as James's was pale and straight—but in the matter of temperament as well. Whereas he himself was a bit of a dreamer, albeit a secret one, James was also rather serious-minded. Seamus, on the other hand, seemed almost completely ungrounded, prone to wildly imaginative flights of fancy. Within minutes of meeting James he was already prattling eagerly on and on about a variety of complicated and confusing conspiracy theories—something about a group called the Illuminati being involved in the revolution in France fifty years earlier, a failed plot against James I back near the time of the first settlements in the New World, a sixteenth-century man named Nostradamus who had predicted the end of the world, and still more that James did not even attempt to follow.

"Look, they are preparing to install something into the cornerstone! Your cousin's passenger told me of this," Seamus cried, startling James. The other boy was pointing to where some men were moving toward the expanse of white marble. "He said it's a case made of zinc, which holds a number of things, including copies of the Declaration of Independence and the Constitution, and also our national flag, a portrait of President Washington, er . . ." He grinned sheepishly and shrugged. "I forget what else. But many interesting items." Standing on tiptoe, Seamus craned his neck for a better view. "Why do you suppose they are doing it, though?"

"Just as a memento, I suppose," James answered without much interest.

"Perhaps, perhaps." Seamus stroked his narrow chin. "I wonder if that Winthrop fellow is a Freemason? They say that President Polk is a member of the order, along with many others in the government."

"Why are you so interested in the Freemasons?" James asked, realizing that Seamus had mentioned the well-known fraternal organization several times already in their short acquaintance. "Does it have something to do with the late President Adams and his anti-Mason party of a few years back?" There had been quite a bit of renewed talk of John Quincy Adams's involvement in the anti-Masonic cause upon the former president's death a few months earlier. James didn't pay much attention to politics, but from what he understood, Adams and the others had believed the Freemasons to be a secret society intent on taking over the government, even though many of the nation's very founders had been Masons.

"Not exactly." Seamus answered. "My interest extends far beyond mere politics, my friend." His dark eyes flashed with excitement. "Didn't you ever hear of William Morgan, the scourge of the Freemasons?"

James glanced around, hoping that no one standing nearby would take offense at Seamus's comments. He wasn't being particularly quiet, and he had stated that the Freemasons were hosting this event. "Isn't he that fellow who disappeared a while back up in New York somewhere?"

he asked, vaguely recalling his father and Thomas making some mention of the incident. "As in, before either of us were born?"

"Indeed. Mr. Morgan was an avowed anti-Mason well before Adams took up the cause." Seamus was practically quivering with excitement as he spoke. "Back in Twenty-six, Morgan planned to publish a book that would expose the secret workings of the Masonic movement. Some members of the local lodge heard about it and took out advertisements against him, and—well, let us just say they made their displeasure known in other, more illicit ways as well." He shrugged. "Then, on September the eleventh of that year, Mr. Morgan was arrested upon accusations by several Masons that he owed them money. He somehow managed to get himself released, but disappeared soon after leaving the jailhouse. An unidentified body was later found in Lake Ontario. It was said by some to be Morgan, but the body was finally identified as belonging to a Canadian man. So nobody truly knows what might have become of Mr. Morgan—though it seems quite clear to me that the Freemasons were involved in his disappearance in one way or another."

"That may be true. But I have heard he is still alive," a new voice observed.

Startled, James glanced over his shoulder to see who had spoken. To his surprise, he immediately recognized the smooth-faced youth from a few minutes earlier. Apparently he had followed them in their attempt to get closer to the stage.

"Is that so?" Seamus asked the stranger eagerly. "Do tell! What do you know of this matter, friend?"

The youth stepped closer, glancing around as if to ascertain that no one else was taking any notice of their conversation. "It is said in some quarters that the disappearance was merely a publicity stunt intended to drum up interest in Mr. Morgan's book, and that he has in fact taken himself off to the West."

"Yes, I have heard that theory myself." Seamus puffed out his thin chest. "We tend to keep up on all the latest news in New York City, where I come from."

"Indeed?" the stranger said. "Well, then perhaps you are also aware that Morgan's so-called widow, Lucinda, later became one of the wives of Joseph Smith, Jr., the founder of the Mormon Church—and a Freemason, himself."

"Of course, though some are determined to deny it to this day," Seamus responded. "I also know that some believe the Freemasons were directly involved in Smith's assassination four years ago."

"Oh?" The other youth blinked, momentarily taken aback. Then he shrugged. "Well, I know nothing of that. It sounds rather speculative. But I shall not say such a thing is impossible, either. Everyone knows of the violent anti-Mormon sentiment that caused Smith's followers to flee Illinois after his death. It is little wonder if the Masons saw the disadvantage in further aligning themselves with that church."

James had little knowledge of, and even less interest in, the subject they were discussing. Who cared what had become of some anti-Mason fellow before any of them were born, or what connection he or his wife or widow might or might not have with the new Mormon movement of the past two decades? To his mind, it seemed much like one of his father's treasure hunts, without even the promise of riches at the other end.

"Returning to what *I* was saying," the stranger went on, "it is this connection between Mr. Morgan and the

Mormons that gave rise to the idea that Morgan might have followed Lucinda out to Illinois or Iowa or elsewhere in the West."

"Interesting indeed. I shall have to look into that. By the way," Seamus said to the stranger, "I am Seamus F. Poole of New York, and this is my new friend, James Gates of Carrollton Manor."

The other youth inclined his head slightly toward the two of them in turn. "My friends call me Sam," he said. "So, Mr. Poole, if you come from New York, what are you doing here?"

Seamus explained the reasons behind his recent arrival. "My father worries overmuch about such things," he added breezily with a wave of one skinny hand. "He was not raised in the city, you see, but spent much of his life in the rural outskirts of Concord, Massachusetts, working at a livery stable. He only moved to New York to marry my dear, departed mother, which happened just a year or so before I came along. Being New York born and raised myself, I am not so nervous of things as my father is."

"I see." Sam pursed his lips. "So being New York born

and raised offers protection from the ravages of cholera, does it?"

James shot the youth a quick glance, wondering if he was having fun with Seamus. Before he could make any determination, Seamus was speaking again.

"Indeed, I was reluctant to leave New York at this time particularly," he said. "You see, I have recently heard that gold has been discovered in the wild western hills of California. I am most interested in hearing more of this matter, and where better than in my bustling city?"

"Gold?" James echoed, feeling a spark of interest in the discussion at last. More than once, he'd entertained fantasies of making his way south to the North Georgia Mountains to seek his fortune in the gold mines, though he generally considered such thoughts no more than idle daydreams, especially now that it was said most of the gold there already had been found. "Do tell—can this be really true?" he added.

"It seems unlikely," Sam put in, his tone dismissive. "There has been no significant gold discovered within the borders of this country since the Georgia Gold Rush twenty years ago."

"That's as may be." Seamus shrugged. "I am merely reporting what I have heard. Not all rumors end up being true. Then again, not all end up being false, either. I won't say I haven't given thought to heading west to see what I might find. Could be worth the gamble."

This time Sam chuckled aloud, surveying Seamus's wiry physique. "I think the greater gamble might be in seeing how long a citified fellow such as yourself could last in the wilds of the Western territories."

James tensed. Had any brand-new acquaintance teased Will thusly, a fight would be almost guaranteed. Luckily, Seamus merely grinned in response.

"Do not doubt me, my friend," he warned Sam playfully. "Else I shall not share my wealth when I am the richest man in the nation."

Relieved, James touched Seamus on the arm. "Come along," he said. "We ought to return to the coach. My brother Thomas does not like to wait, and if he gets there before us, he shall be insufferable afterward."

"Oh, but we have barely begun to talk to Sam here!" Seamus protested. "I was hoping to delve more into the Morgan case, as it appears we both share an interest in it."

"Never mind," Sam said. "Perhaps we can carry on the discussion via letter. You said you shall be staying with Mr. Gates at Carrollton Manor, yes?"

Seamus nodded eagerly. "Why don't you give me your address as well?" he suggested.

"Er, that will not be necessary." Sam smiled and took a few steps backward. "I shall write to you shortly, never fear. It is always a pleasure to make a new acquaintance with an open mind."

"But . . ." Seamus began, to no avail. With only a last wave of his slim, pale hand, Sam melted away into the crowd.

"He's an odd one, isn't he?" James commented. "Sounded almost as if he didn't want us to know much about him."

Seamus shrugged. "Are you sure we need to leave now?" he asked, glancing around. "I haven't had a chance to speak with any Masons. Now that I know that others hold the theory that Mr. Morgan might still be alive, I have more interest than ever in looking into the matter further."

"It shall have to wait, I'm afraid," James said firmly. He couldn't help thinking that perhaps it was for the best after all that he'd been sent on this trip, as he suspected that while Thomas might have more interest than he in some of Seamus's conspiacy theories, he would have little patience for the newcomer's constant chatter. "Come, let's find our way back to the coach."

Two

Some weeks later, James sat in an empty stall in his family's ramshackle barn shuffling through the letters in his lap. Things had been busy since his sister's wedding, and he'd had only a few brief chances to look at them until now. Those early glances had showed that all the letters in the packet were indeed from his aunt, dating from the early days of her marriage up until less than a year ago.

Now he set about putting them in order according to the dates she'd carefully scripted at the top of each page. A twinge of guilt distracted him at first—he couldn't imagine what his father might say if he knew his youngest son was reading his private correspondence—but he did his best to put that out of his mind. It was too late for such qualms now.

The early letters were interesting in their own way, providing a glimpse into Ellie's travels with her explorer husband, Richard, news of the birth of their children, and later the sad news of Richard's death. But it was the last few missives that had caught James's attention upon closer reading. Each of them contained, among the ordinary news and gossip, a few lines of verse. His gaze lingered over the earliest of these, dated in late 1840. The lines read:

> Dare ye seek to take your measure
> By heading West after dearest Treasure?
> Mark these letters; pay close mind
> And p'raps this Treasure ye shall find.

James's expression darkened as he read over the second line again: *dearest Treasure.* . . . .Was it true then that it was not only his father and brother who remained obsessed with the fruitless quest for treasure? For a moment, he was tempted to crumple the letter in his hand and toss it away to be swept out with the stall's soiled bedding. This foolish quest for treasure had caused so much heartbreak in his family. . . .

But he couldn't resist imagining another, much more enticing possibility. Just because Aunt Ellie had used the word treasure, it did not necessarily mean she was referring to something like the mythical Lost City of Gold or the legendary Treasure of the Ancients, which his father and Thomas were constantly discussing in hushed tones. From everything he had heard of her, she seemed far too sensible for that. For all he knew, she could be speaking of something far more tangible.

He blinked as the idea took hold in his mind. Could it be? After all, Seamus was still chattering to all who would listen about the gold he'd heard about out in California, where Aunt Ellie now made her home. And James had heard from his older brothers that Adam and Ellie had in their youth enjoyed confounding each other with all manner of codes and riddles. What if Aunt Ellie had sent her brother a coded set of clues to some riches she had discovered in the wilds of the western lands, whether something like gold or perhaps an inheritance from her recently deceased husband that she wished to share with the family?

That wouldn't really be a treasure hunt of the sort that would normally interest Father, he told himself. *True, on the surface it seems to share some qualities with the Charlotte clue, but it could be seen as something more like a real map—a set of instructions to find something that is definitely there, coded in such a way that others would not discern her meaning in case the letters were to be intercepted on their way to Father.* He clutched the edges of the letter a little tighter. *Even though travel to the West is risky and difficult, it would still be a much surer path to wealth than some vague, impossible clue regarding an unknown personage named Charlotte, allegedly leading to some vast, impossible treasure left by a boodle of secretive—and, at least according to what Seamus says, unreliable—Freemasons. . . .*

His heart quickened as he sat there imagining it. What if it were true? What if he was holding in his hands the key to the freedom and respect of which he'd always dreamed?

Knowing in the more sensible part of his mind that he was only giving in to wishful thinking, he nevertheless could not resist turning to the next letter, hoping to find some more definitive answer there. But before he could scan to find the next verse, there came a sudden loud clatter in the aisle just outside. James barely had time to hide the letters in his shirt before Seamus burst into the stall, breathless and wide-eyed.

"There you are, James!" he cried with a grin. "I've been searching all over for you."

"What is it?" James stood up, brushing bits of chaff off his pants. Although Seamus had quickly made himself at home in the Gates household, James still hadn't quite grown fully accustomed to his boisterous presence.

At the moment, Seamus was practically bubbling over with excitement. "It's true," he exclaimed. "I told you so— it's true!"

"What's true?" James inquired, wondering which of Seamus's various tall tales and bizarre theories he believed he had confirmed.

"Look here—it's in the *New York Herald*. See for yourself!"

At first glance, the newspaper Seamus was waving seemed to contain little more than the usual stories and political cartoons revolving around the upcoming presidential election among Whig Zachary Taylor, Democrat Lewis Cass, and former president Martin Van Buren of the recently formed Free Soil Party. But when James grabbed it for a better look, he soon spotted tucked in among the other articles one confirming that gold had been discovered in California and that citizens of that region were even now making their fortunes in a matter of hours or days.

"Well, dash it all!" James exclaimed as he read through the article, stepping out of the stall toward the open stable doors for better light. "So it *is* true!"

His mind immediately wandered back over the daydreams of prosperity brought on by his aunt's letters. Even if his guess as to the meaning of her verses was wrong, it seemed there was a fortune to be made out west after all. . . .

"What is it?" Seamus peered into his face. "You have an odd look about you, James."

"Nothing." Shaking off such thoughts, James handed the newspaper back to Seamus. "I am merely impressed that your news has proven true, that's all."

"Indeed." Seamus smiled in a satisfied way. Then his smile faded a bit as he glanced at the paper in his hand. "Though I don't know what good it does me, stuck here in the States as I am." He brightened again. "Oh! But did I tell you I've had a letter from that fellow Sam we met on July Fourth? He wanted to know if I'd heard anything more about the gold—seemed quite interested, actually, despite his earlier dismissal. Wanted to know if I was just bragging before when I talked of going out there. Even provided a return address at a tavern in Baltimore city so that I might write him back." He grinned. "Wait until I tell him of this!"

"Hmm." Before James could respond further, there came

a call from the stable yard just outside. A moment later, a tall, ginger-haired man of around thirty years old peered into the barn.

"Hello," the man greeted them in a friendly manner. "Might I trouble you to tell me where I can find the proprietor of this livery? I am looking to hire passage."

"I can help you, sir." James stepped forward. "I'm James Gates. My father owns this stable."

"Ah, excellent." The man held out his hand to shake. "My name is Meriwether Clark. I've been traveling in the area and now need passage back to St. Louis. I wish to depart in about a week's time."

"Meriwether Clark?" Seamus, who had been looking down at his newspaper, now suddenly jerked his head up and hurried forward to join them. "You would not be Meriwether *Lewis* Clark, son of the great explorer William Clark, who led the first expedition across the entire continent to the far western coast in the early days of this century?"

"Indeed I am." Mr. Clark inclined his head politely. "My late father named me after his friend and partner on that journey, Captain Meriwether Lewis."

"It is an honor and a pleasure to meet you, sir!" Seamus grabbed the man's hand and shook it vigorously. "Truly, Mr. Clark, an honor!"

James shot him a look. Indeed, most people alive knew of the explorations of Lewis and Clark. But why was Seamus making such a fuss out of a chance meeting with one of the explorers' sons? Was this another of his personal quirks, similar to being so fascinated with conspiracy and mystery?

Such questions fled his mind instantly when he heard Seamus's next comment: "And of course, Mr. Clark, we will be honored to carry you to St. Louis next week! You need only name the time you wish to depart."

"Wonderful!" Mr. Clark beamed at him, then at James. "I shall write down the address where I am staying in Baltimore. Shall you be able to pick me up there?"

"Absolutely," Seamus assured him. "It is no trouble at all, sir."

James felt frozen in horror. The family's hack business currently had only two coaches, both of which were needed frequently for local journeys. There was no way his father would allow one of them to be away long enough for a round trip journey to faraway St. Louis!

But before he could come up with a tactful way to say as much, Mr. Clark had tipped his hat and departed. As soon as he was gone, James whirled to face Seamus.

"Are you feebleminded?" he cried. "Why did you agree to such a deal as that?"

Seamus seemed not to notice his ire. He was staring off in the direction Mr. Clark had gone, a satisfied expression on his face.

"William Clark was well known to be a Freemason," he said. "In fact, he was first initiated into the lodge in St. Louis that his friend Captain Lewis helped found. What do you suppose are the chances that his son is a member of the order as well?" He stroked his chin, looking thoughtful. "I suppose it is of little matter either way. Surely he knows much of the Brotherhood even if only through his father. And the long journey to St. Louis should give me plenty of time to coax out of him whatever he might know."

James stared at him. "Wait," he said. "You mean you committed one of our coaches without asking Father only due to this strange obsession of yours with the Freemasons?"

"That's not the only reason, my friend." Seamus rolled up the newspaper he was holding and waved it at him.

"Don't you see? This could be our chance! We need only to convince your father and Arthur that we should be the ones to deliver Mr. Clark to St. Louis. Once we're that far west, perhaps we shall be able to find out more firm information about that California gold!"

James frowned. He suspected that Seamus had no idea of the true distance between the western frontier in Missouri and the distant reaches of coastal California. But that was hardly the point.

"There will be no convincing," he said shortly. "As soon as he hears of this, Father will have your head and then there'll be no chance of gold for you at all."

And indeed, when Adam first heard the news, he was outraged. "How dare you?" he cried, staring wide-eyed at Seamus and James. "You know we cannot spare a coach for so long at one time! It is madness!"

"I understand, Uncle Adam," Seamus protested. "But if you had met the charming Mr. Clark yourself, I am sure—"

"Hold it." Adam held up one hand. "Is he—might he be relation to the late William Clark, by chance?"

Seamus nodded. "Indeed he is—he is the man's own son, Meriwether."

James gazed in surprise at his father, whose expression had suddenly changed from anger to a sort of confused wonder. Had the whole world gone mad? What was it about this Meriwether Clark that could cause people to react in such extraordinary ways? He had certainly seemed ordinary enough to James.

Meanwhile Adam was shaking his head. "Ah, the son of Captain Clark," he said, his voice twinged with awe—and James thought—nostalgia. "Well then, I suppose if you've already agreed to this job, we shouldn't back out now. We shall have to make do with the single coach for a while, that is all." Suddenly seeming to snap out of his reverie, he resumed glaring at the pair. "However, I am quite certain that the others shall have little interest in making the long and arduous journey to Missouri. As you two are the ones who got us into this, you shall be the ones to make the trip and deliver Mr. Clark to his destination."

James opened his mouth to protest—*he* had not been the one to agree to the job! In fact, he'd known it to be a mistake and had done his best to stop it!

But as his father turned away, James shut his mouth again without speaking, guessing that such explanations would do no good. Once again, he was the expendable one, the one being sent off to do the job nobody else wanted.

He frowned after his father's departing back, hardly hearing Seamus chattering eagerly beside him about the coming adventure. *Perhaps I should just keep heading west from St. Louis as Seamus suggests,* he thought, feeling rebellious. *I could solve those clues from Aunt Ellie's letter and track down whatever valuables she's referring to, and if that didn't work out, perhaps mine for some of that gold in California and make my fortune that way. . . .*

Then his shoulders slumped as he realized he would never have the gumption to do anything of the sort. Besides, it would do little to change his father's feelings toward him. He doubted anyone would notice or miss him. They would only wonder what had become of the coach and horses, forgetting he'd ever been there at all.

Three

"Good day, sir." James hoisted the package he was holding. "I have this delivery for you from Point of Rocks."

"Thank you, m'boy." The recipient of the delivery, a stout man dressed in a velvet waistcoat and satin cravat, reached into his pocket for a coin, which he flipped to James. "There's a little something for your trouble."

As the man disappeared behind the door of his fine townhome, James stared down at the coin in his hand. A little something, indeed. Would he ever be the one carelessly tossing coins to delivery boys rather than the one catching them? Not so long as he was stuck running annoying errands such as this for the cussed Arthur, that much was certain.

He climbed back into the coach and picked up the reins, clucking to the horses. Knowing how little good it did to brood over such matters, he turned his mind to the subject of his aunt's letters. Two days had passed since that private moment in the stall, and in that time he'd committed the second verse from his aunt's letters to memory. He thought of it now as the coach rumbled over the cobblestoned streets of Baltimore city.

Where our joyful old friend
had his last stand;
Begin to Trace your journey
out across the land.

What could it mean? He had already theorized that the first verse might merely be a way to introduce the quest. This second clue—if that was indeed what it was—seemed similar in theme but more cryptic. Was there some hidden meaning there that could lead him one step closer to financial reward?

Before he could decide, James spotted several swine sleeping in the narrow city street just ahead, blocking the way. Muttering under his breath, he stopped the horses and climbed down to awaken the pigs and shoo them out of the way. As he did so, he noticed a bit of paper fluttering from a wall nearby. The large number printed in boldface at the top, along with the word REWARD!, caught his attention, and he stepped closer for a look.

The flyer was offering a substantial reward for information as to the whereabouts of a Miss Sally Chandler, the seventeen-year-old daughter of a local resident, who had been missing for some two months. *"Help save our daughter's soul by reporting any sightings to her anxious family,"* the plea continued. *"Believed to be hiding her transgressions from us in the greater Baltimore region. All queries and information shall be appreciated and rewarded as qualified."* Below the text was a drawing of the missing girl in question, followed by the name and address of her father.

James took down the flyer and stared closely at the sketch for a moment. It was quite detailed, and he couldn't help thinking there was something strangely familiar about Miss Chandler's face.

Then one of the horses snorted and stamped its foot, reminding James that the shadows were already growing longer and that Arthur would be in a snit if he were late returning to Carrollton Manor. With a sigh, James pocketed the flyer and hurried back to the coach.

Even as he took up the reins once more, he was imagining

what it would be like to be the owner of the sum mentioned in that reward. It would be enough to start him on his own in life—or at least allow him to refuse to heed his brother-in-law's every whim—and perhaps even prove to his family that he shouldn't be ignored.

If James had felt underappreciated before, things had only grown worse as Arthur began to fancy himself in complete charge of the hack business. Adam and Thomas were far too distracted by their latest theories about the mysterious Charlotte to notice that he was taking over, and Will and Sam, who had always been friendly with Arthur, seemed not to mind. It was no wonder, since they were never the ones ordered to do the most menial or unpleasant jobs. Even Seamus seemed unbothered by Arthur's bossiness, despite being nearly as likely as James to be assigned the tasks nobody else wanted. Perhaps this was because everything was all so new to him, or perhaps it was due to his generally sunny nature.

In any case, the brunt of the burden once again seemed to have fallen on James. And he wasn't sure how much longer he could bear it.

✳ ✳ ✳

The next day brought a harbinger of the coming autumn, with patchy gray skies and fitful cloudbursts throughout the morning. James spent most of the hours after breakfast sorting buckles in the barn's gloomy tack room. This dull work lulled him quickly into a near stupor, which was broken only at the sound of an outraged roar from the stable yard.

He hurried outside to find Arthur standing there, a deep scowl on his red, puffy face. "What is the meaning of this?" he shouted.

James gulped. He had quickly seen what had infuriated his brother-in-law. A bunch of harness leather lay piled in the courtyard, showing signs of having been there through the day's latest set of rain showers.

"I see why you are upset," he told Arthur, keeping his voice steady. "But you need not yell at me. I had nothing to do with leaving the harness out here."

"Indeed?" Arthur glared at him, arms akimbo. "Then tell me *who* I should blame? Willie was with me until just now, and Sam left with the small coach for Hagerstown this morning. I've seen neither hide nor hair of Thomas all day, nor your father, either. If you didn't do it, who did? One of the horses, perhaps?"

James rolled his eyes at the sarcasm, though he didn't say anything. He had a pretty good idea just who was responsible for the rain-soaked harness—Seamus. Now that he thought of it, James remembered that Seamus had wandered through the tack room some time earlier, saying something about cleaning some tack outdoors in the fresh air while the sun was briefly shining.

"Well?" Arthur folded his arms across his chest, still glaring. "What do you have to say for yourself, boy? I've let quite a bit of irresponsible behavior pass lately, but this is too much. Ruined harness costs money." He shook his head and curled his lip. "Not that I'd expect a Gates to understand that," he added under his breath.

James wanted to lash back, to tell his hateful brother-in-law in no uncertain terms that he was mistaken—that *this* Gates, at least, had as much sense of money as Arthur himself, if not more. And his sense of fairness cried out at the very notion of accepting the blame for something he had not done. Still, James was not the type of person to pin blame on another who had not harmed him, no matter how tempting it might be. So after a brief internal struggle, he merely shrugged and kept quiet.

Arthur took the silence as acknowledgment of guilt. He raised a finger, about to start on another speech, when Seamus appeared in the barn doorway.

The boy's eyes widened as he took in the sight of the soaked leather. "Oh!" Seamus exclaimed. "The harness got wet!"

"Indeed it did, for that is what happens when some fool leaves it out in the rain," Arthur growled. "And James here will pay for it one way or another, I reckon."

"But it's not his fault—it's mine," Seamus explained. "I'm sorry. I went to the pump for a drink of water and forgot entirely what I'd been doing."

Arthur shot him a look, his small, round eyes briefly registering a sort of dull confusion. Then he shrugged. "Good try, boy," he snapped. "Figures that you and the other one would try to cover for each other. Very well. If you like, I'll punish the both of you."

"What?" James exclaimed. "But listen, he's already apologized, and it's not as if the harness is truly ruined—a good oiling is all it will take for it to be good as new. Besides, what right have you to punish either of us? We are not your naughty children!"

"Enough!" Arthur cut him off. "You two are incorrigible. Why was it that nobody bothered to mention to me until this morning that the pair of you has committed one of our coaches for some dandy's trip to St. Louis?"

James gulped, realizing that his increasingly absent-minded father must have neglected to fill in Arthur until now. "Father approved it," he said, unable to keep all the resentment out of his voice. "I don't see that it's your place to question his decision."

"Oh, don't you?" Arthur took a step closer. "Well perhaps you can think it over while you fix this leather. But you'd best finish it within the next two days, because it's the two of you who shall be making the long, hot, dusty drive all the way to the western edge of the States. You made the promise, *you* can fulfill it."

Although that was much the same way his father had put it, it seemed somehow even worse coming from the imperious Arthur. "Oh, is that so?" James retorted, feeling his face go red. "Well—"

"Never mind." Seamus silenced him with a look. "We

understand, Arthur. And we'll get right to work on the harness."

"See that you do." Then Arthur spun on the heel of his heavy brogans and stomped off into the barn.

"Sorry about that, James." Seamus bent and started gathering the wet harness off the ground and looping it over his skinny arms. "This mess is my fault. Arthur shouldn't have blamed you."

"Thanks." A little surprised by Seamus's sincere apology, James stepped over to help pick up the harness. "But whereas this wet leather may be your doing, it is no fault of yours that my brother-in-law happens to be a cussed scalawag."

Seamus shrugged. "In any case, I hope you do not mind the bit about the drive out west," he said, the usual gleam coming into his eyes. "I think it shall be quite an adventure."

"Perhaps," James replied with a sigh. "If only I could figure out Aunt Ellie's clues, we could at least make it a profitable adventure."

"What?" Seamus demanded. "What clues do you mean? Who is Aunt Ellie? Do you mean the Ellie who was with our fathers on their own western adventure all those years ago?"

James winced. He'd spoken without thinking. Still, what harm would it do to tell Seamus about the letters? Nobody else in the family paid much attention to either of them, so he wasn't likely to give away the secret—even by accident. So, after swearing Seamus to secrecy, he filled him in.

"Fascinating!" Seamus said when James was done. "So you believe your aunt's letters may be offering a clue to some hidden treasure?"

"*Not* treasure," James said quickly. "Not the way my father and brother mean it, anyway. No, I figure it's probably money, or perhaps a gold vein or some such. Otherwise, why would she not have revealed it sooner? I'm sure she only coded it so nobody else could steal the valuables if they saw the letters. Or maybe it is something valuable only to a Gates. In any case, it seems worth following up, does it not? I feel confident I could work out the meaning of those verses given enough time." He grimaced. "Which we will have on our trip."

"True enough," Seamus agreed. "And while we're at it, perhaps we can try to track down the missing Mr. Morgan as well—after all, it's said he is somewhere in the wilds of the west. Did I mention that I had another letter from our new friend Sam today? He says—"

"That's it!" James blurted out, his eyes suddenly going wide as a jolt passed through his body.

Seamus looked confused. "That's what?" he said. "I haven't even told you what he's said yet."

"Sorry." James busied himself by looking down at the harness he was holding, doing his best to hide a growing sense of excitement. "Er, go on. What were you saying?"

Seamus shrugged and continued talking. But James barely heard a word of it. Perhaps he wouldn't need to concern himself with rumored gold mines or perplexing clues after all. Perhaps he had just hit upon a way to make his fortune—right there in Maryland!

Four

James looked from the numbers on the door of the house before him back down to the paper in his hand, then up again. This was it—the address matched. He gazed at the house, clearly one of the largest in this section of Baltimore. The genteel neighborhood was much quieter and its streets less crowded than neighboring areas, the fine carriages rumbling past now and then making the well-worn saddle on the horse James had ridden to town look rather shabby. He felt self-conscious and out of place just being there, though he did his best to push such thoughts aside. Soon, if all went well, he would have more than enough money to belong anywhere he pleased.

He glanced once more at the paper in his hand. It was the flyer he'd pocketed on the previous day, the one advertising the ample reward for information on the missing Sally Chandler. Tucking it away again in his clothes, James took a deep breath and then started up the steps. Tugging at the bell pull, he stepped back and waited, his heart pounding nervously.

A moment later the door swung open, revealing an immaculately dressed butler with slicked-back hair and a small mustache. The man peered at him suspiciously down a rather prominent nose.

"Can I help you, young man?" the butler asked.

"My name is James Madison Gates of Carrollton Manor. I am here to see Mr. Chandler." James squared his shoulders, trying to look officious and mature. "I may have news that he would like to hear."

"Mr. Chandler is a very busy man."

"I understand. And I am not here to waste his time." Now that his salvation was so close, James was not going to allow this butler—or his own nerves—to turn him away. "I may have news for him regarding his missing daughter, Sally."

The butler's expression changed to that of great concern. "I see," he said soberly. "Wait here, if you please. I shall see if Mr. Chandler is available."

A few minutes later James was being ushered along a wallpapered hallway illuminated with the latest style of gaslights and into a richly appointed sitting room. James's eyes were drawn immediately to several daguerreotype pictures of a pretty, smiling, pale-haired girl. There was no question that she was the same young lady from that sketch—the missing Sally Chandler. The daguerreotypes also left little doubt in James's mind that he had not been mistaken in coming here.

A broad-shouldered, burly man of about fifty with a wide, flat face and bushy sideburns rose from behind a large rosewood desk. "I hear you bring news of Sally," he said without preamble.

James cleared his throat and nodded as the butler faded away, closing the door behind him. "Indeed, I believe your daughter to be in contact with a member of my household," he said. "I also believe that I made her acquaintance myself some time ago, though I had no idea of her true identity at the time."

"I see. And what identity did she present to you?" Mr. Chandler asked, stepping from behind his desk and coming toward him with an expression of intense interest.

"She was—" James hesitated, not sure how to phrase the answer without offending the man. "Er, she was . . ."

"Spit it out, boy." Chandler sounded rather impatient. "How has she disguised her identity this time?"

Squaring his shoulders, James decided there was little choice but to state plainly what he knew. "I believe she was dressed as a—as a boy, sir," he said, feeling his cheeks go pink. "At the time of our meeting, I fully believed her to be a young gentleman by the name of Sam."

The older man blew out a loud sigh. "Indeed, that sounds like our Sally," he said grimly, little surprised by James's revelation. "I am ashamed to say that she has adopted all manner of unseemly behavior these past few years, despite our best efforts to mold her into a young lady of character. Dressing as a boy is not even the worst of it, believe it or not. That is why it is so urgent that we find her and bring her home before she causes further harm to herself or to others."

James swallowed hard, wishing to ask for clarification but not quite daring. Sam—if indeed he was truly this Sally Chandler—had seemed pleasant and intelligent enough. What could she possibly have done to cause her family so much consternation? And why, if her family cared so much, would she have run away?

Mr. Chandler started pacing the room, arms behind his back and an expression of concentration upon his face. "You say she is in contact with someone in your household," he said. Stopping abruptly and turning to stare at James, he added, "Do you think you can arrange a meeting? If I can get hold of her, get her back under the influence of the family, I am sure there is some hope for her yet."

James blinked and took a step back. He had not been expecting this. He had a good feeling that there was more to the story of Sally Chandler. "Er, I do not know," he hedged uneasily. "That is, I had not anticipated being so directly involved. I had only thought, after seeing your advertisement I mean . . ."

"Ah, I understand now." The man frowned briefly, then spun on his heel and hurried back over to the desk. Digging into one of the drawers, he soon came up with a handful of bills and coins. "Here you are then. I shall give you twenty percent of the reward now as a show of good faith. The rest will be forthcoming after Sally is once more safely at home with us."

James's eyes widened as the man pressed the money into his hands. He couldn't remember the last time he'd set eyes on this much cash all at once, let alone been the owner of it. And there was more to come! All he had to do was betray Sally to get it.

But what loyalty do I owe her, after all? he asked himself. *She lied to me about her true identity and to Seamus, too. And I really haven't spent much time with her. . . .*

He gulped, briefly wondering what Seamus would say when he learned of this. But he reassured himself by thinking again of Mr. Chandler's rather mysterious comment about his daughter's "unseemly behavior." Maybe his gut was wrong. If Sally was truly a danger to herself or others, he would be doing a good thing by helping return her to the custody of her family. Besides that, the reward money could change his life. With it, there would no longer be need for him to daydream of some hardscrabble fortune that might possibly be won in the untamed West. He would have enough to make a new life for himself right here and now in the States.

"All right," he blurted out before he could change his mind. "I'll see what I can do. But it shall have to be very soon—I leave for St. Louis in two days' time."

"The sooner the better." Mr. Chandler rubbed his hands

together, seeming satisfied. "I'll await your message. And thank you, young man."

A moment later James found himself back on the street outside the Chandler home, his head spinning with what had just transpired. He mounted his horse and rode slowly toward the nearest intersection. When he reached the corner, he passed a group of young men talking loudly in the street.

". . . and they say people are making their way to California from all over the world to try to make their fortunes!" one was saying in a tone of great excitement, waving his arms about. "I read it in the papers—this gold is real! Do you wish to miss it? I say we leave as soon as we can and head overland! By train if we can."

"All the gold in the world shall do us no good if we end up like nearly half that unfortunate Donner party did this past winter," one of his companions pointed out. "Did you not read of *that* in the papers? No, much better we should wait until spring to set out."

"But then we shall not be able to start mining until a year hence! By then, the gold might be gone!" the first young man argued.

"I say we strike a compromise," a third man suggested.

"We could depart for Illinois immediately so as not to waste any time, outfit ourselves there, and stay the winter before heading west as soon as the weather permits."

"Why should we not travel by sea?" yet another member of the group spoke up. "That would allow us to leave immediately, and they say it is the easiest way to reach the far coast. . . ."

By now James was too far past the little group to hear any more. But he found himself thinking over the young men's discussion. It was obvious that they were would-be Argonauts hoping to head west in search of that gold Seamus kept talking about.

His mind drifted to Aunt Ellie's clues, particularly that second one over which he had been puzzling as of late. What "joyful old friend" could she mean in the first line? Might it have something to do with her own dear old friend Franklin Poole, Seamus's father? After all, if father were anything like son, he could surely be described as "joyful."

But James shook off the thought, telling himself that those clues were now of as little importance as the California gold. What need had he anymore of risky ventures to the West? He would complete the trip to St. Louis out of a sense of responsibility to Mr. Clark and Seamus. But after that, back home again with Mr. Chandler's reward money in hand, he would be ready to begin his new life—out from under Arthur's rule and the Gates's family obsession.

Five

Two days later, James found himself once more in Baltimore, and once more he was feeling nervous. So far, his plan seemed to be working. He had convinced Seamus to contact "Sam" via urgent letter—the delivery paid for out of the down payment on the reward money, though Seamus did not know that, of course—and invite "him" to meet with them in Baltimore this morning. James was a bit uneasy about the timing, as they were due to collect Mr. Clark at his place of lodging shortly afterward. However, there had not been enough time to arrange a meeting with Sam/Sally the previous day and besides, both coaches and most of the horses had been busy. So they would have to make do as the situation stood, tight timing notwithstanding.

As of yet, Seamus had no idea of the true reason behind the meeting with his new friend Sam. He was under the assumption they were to share the letters from Aunt Ellie. That had been the first explanation that had popped into

James's head while suggesting the plan, and luckily Seamus seemed to find it a perfectly credible reason for fitting the encounter into their already busy day. In fact, he had spent most of the ride to the city chattering about the various possible treasures to which the letters might be pointing them, to the extent that he had begun to sound almost like Adam and Thomas.

"Perhaps we can convince Sam to come along with us to St. Louis," Seamus was saying as they drove slowly through a congested area of the city. "I realize we do not know his family situation, or what responsibilities he might have to keep him here in Baltimore. But if he does happen to be free to depart on a whim, I feel certain that Mr. Clark would not mind the extra companionship." He grinned at James. "With any luck, our friend Sam might be able to help me wheedle some useful information out of the esteemed Mr. Clark during the course of our lengthy journey. After all, Sam seems to know nearly as much about the Freemasons as I do myself. And if we are moving farther west after St. Louis in search of gold and treasure, we might as well have a look for William Morgan as well, yes?"

James smiled weakly, not bothering to answer, especially

since Seamus was already launching into a soliloquy involving his latest speculations about the long-missing Mr. Morgan. Even though the rational part of his mind knew that this was all for the best, James still couldn't help feeling vaguely guilty about what they were about to do—*if* they managed to pull it off. So much depended on everything happening at just the right time. If Sam/Sally happened to be delayed by even a few minutes, the whole plan would fall apart. He felt a bit more confident that Mr. Chandler would be there at the appointed time, eager as he was to retrieve his wayward daughter as soon as possible. Still, there was little he could do either way other than play his own role and hope for the best.

He squinted upward, checking the position of the sun. "We shall have to be quick about this," he said, speaking as much to himself as to Seamus. "We are due to pick up Mr. Clark at his boardinghouse just a quarter hour or so after our meeting with, er, Sam." He nearly stumbled over the name, remembering at the last minute not to refer to "Sally" in front of Seamus.

"I know." Seamus glanced at him with a little frown. "I do not know why you have scheduled our meeting with Sam so close to when we are meant to depart for St. Louis. It will give us little time to convince him to ride along with us, or to talk with him if he cannot."

James didn't bother to enlighten him, but in fact he had the timing of this day planned out as meticulously as possible, considering the complex and difficult circumstances. He originally had wished to make the rendezvous with Sally and her father a little earlier, but Arthur had insisted that he stop at a certain tavern in Baltimore to pick up some mail he was expecting from the North and West, which James was then to drop at another tavern in one of the towns on the road west after collecting Mr. Clark, where it would be more convenient for one of James's brothers to fetch it later that week.

It was tempting to ignore this errand and head straight to the square where they were to meet Sally, especially now that James knew he would not be under Arthur's thumb much longer. But knowing that others in Carrollton Manor might have their important letters delayed through no fault of their own, he resisted the urge and turned the team toward the tavern in question.

"We shall have enough time to discuss what we need to

discuss today," he told Seamus. "Let's pick up the mail, then proceed on foot from here. The meeting spot is only a few blocks away, and that way the horses can have a drink and a rest."

They tied the horses in front of the tavern, collected the mail, and set it safely inside the coach. Then they walked off toward the square, Seamus dancing a bit ahead with eagerness.

"Where is he?" Seamus cried as they entered the square, which was small and dusty, with several large trees casting shade over the nearby buildings. He spun on his heel and stared around. "Oh, I hope he did not mistake the date or time of this meeting!"

James shared that hope. His stomach clenched with worry as he glanced around, searching the face of each passerby. What if Sally did not come? Could she possibly have discovered what was really going on? He couldn't imagine how. But what if she had been delayed, or thought the meeting was next hour, or tomorrow? With Mr. Clark perhaps already waiting for him and Seamus close by, they would not be able to linger. And who knew what could happen in the time it would take him to travel to St. Louis and back? Sally might go home on her own—and he might miss his chance to collect the rest of the reward money. The thought was crushing. How could he return to his life of dreary hopelessness now, when he'd had such a tantalizing taste of other possibilities?

Just then, he noticed a flash of movement out of the corner of his eye. He spun around, hoping to see "Sam" approaching. Instead he caught a glimpse of a ruddy face and bushy sideburns. It was Mr. Chandler; he had just peered out from behind the tree trunk where he was hiding. With a quick nod, he ducked out of sight once again. James gulped, trying not to imagine what the man might say if his daughter did not appear as James had promised. . . .

"There he is!" Seamus shouted in his ear, startling him. "Sam! Over here, my friend!"

Sure enough, James turned and saw "Sam" heading toward them from across the square, wearing a roundabout coat and carrying a well-worn carpetbag. Having now seen the daguerreotype of Sally, it was easy for him to see the familiar lines of a girl's pretty face even beneath the man's hairstyle and hat. How had he and Seamus ever mistaken her for a boy?

"Good morning, fellows," Sam/Sally called back with a smile. "I was surprised to get your message. Are you—"

At that moment, her father leaped into view. "Sally!" he cried.

She gasped, her face instantly growing paler. "Father!" she blurted out.

Then she dropped her bag and turned to flee. But her path was blocked by a large, swarthy-faced man who grabbed her by the arm. She cried out and struggled, but the man was strong and maintained his grip easily. Mr. Chandler was already hurrying toward them, his face grim. Several bystanders stared with open interest at the scene, but none made any move to intervene as Mr. Chandler grabbed his daughter's free arm and shook her while the other man took a step back and watched impassively.

"You dratted girl, causing us such worry!" Chandler yelled directly into his daughter's face. "What do you have to say for yourself? Answer me, Sally!"

"But I don't understand," Seamus cried with obvious confusion. "What is happening? Sam? Who are these men, and who is Sally?"

James tugged at his sleeve, wanting only to get away

from the unpleasant scene. Now that it was done, he felt oddly guilty. He figured he could collect his reward later, once he had returned from St. Louis and things had settled.

"It's no business of ours," he muttered to Seamus. "Come, it is time for us to get back to the coach, or we'll be late."

Meanwhile, another man, this one a sallow-faced dandy-type in his late twenties, had emerged and joined the other two. "Don't get yourself so huffed, Sally darling," he said with a bored sigh, crossing his thin arms over his chest and leaning back against a post. "You need not worry, I shall not hold this ridiculous episode of yours against you. We shall put it all behind us and never speak of it again once we marry."

"I shall never marry you, Winston," Sally spat, her blue eyes flashing with fury. "I do not care how my father may try to force me." Suddenly noticing James and Seamus still standing there, she glared at them as well. "Or my so-called friends, either. I thought I could trust you! I should have known better—it seems no man can ever be trusted!"

James was experiencing a most unpleasant sinking

feeling in his stomach. "Wait," he blurted out, taking a step forward. "Is *that* why you went missing? Because you would not agree to marry this man? I did not know that."

Mr. Chandler shot him an irritated look. "And why should you?" he snapped. "That's family business."

That was true enough. But now that he knew, James could not stop himself flashing to the vision of intelligent, likable Sally being forced to marry someone she so clearly despised.

Family tales always claimed that James's father had been quite impulsive during his younger years. Until this moment, James had always assumed he'd failed to inherit that particular character trait. Careful thought, scrupulous planning—that sort of thing generally suited him better.

But for once, he found himself acting on instinct, with no pause to allow rational thought to adjust his reaction. Bending down, he grabbed a bucket of spoiled milk that someone had left out for the local wandering pigs. In one swift movement, he splashed it directly into Mr. Chandler's face. The man let out a yell, momentarily loosening his hold on his daughter's arm.

Darting forward, James grabbed Sally by the hand.

"Run!" he shouted, yanking her after him.

Seamus was standing slack-jawed. James gave him a shove as he raced past, which seemed to awaken him from his perplexed stupor. Dashing after James and Sally, they headed for the nearest street, pausing just long enough to grab Sally's carpetbag as they passed it.

"How dare you? Stop right there!" Mr. Chandler roared from just behind them. "After them!"

Six

"**F**aster!" James yelled a few moments later as the three of them raced around another corner and came within view of the coach, which was still safely tied in front of the tavern. "Come on!"

He chanced a glance back over his shoulder. Mr. Chandler was less than a block behind them now, sprinting at an impressive pace for such a large man. He was flanked by Sally's intended and the other man. All three of them looked furious.

James gulped, putting on an extra burst of speed. If those men caught them . . .

He didn't dare finish the thought. "Untie the horses!" he shouted to Seamus. Without stopping to make sure the order was obeyed, he grabbed Sally around the waist and hoisted her bodily into the enclosed main box of the coach.

"Eep!" she squeaked out in surprise. But she caught the

edge of the doorway and clambered the rest of the way in without protest.

By now the three pursuers were almost upon them. "Stop right there, boy!" Mr. Chandler howled. "Stop in your tracks if you know what's good for you!"

Ignoring the command, James vaulted onto the open driver's bench and grabbed the reins. By now Seamus had the team loose. The horses, sensing something unusual afoot, had their heads up and ears pricked. The livelier of the two, a lean, Roman-nosed bay, let out a snort and pawed at the cobblestones.

"Go! Go!" Seamus cried, racing back along the right side of the coach. He flung Sally's bag aboard through the open door, then grabbed on to the edge of the seat riser and pulled himself onto the bench beside James.

"Hold on, everyone!" James shouted, cracking the whip over the horses' backs, sending them into a scrambling trot. With a bit of additional urging, they were soon careening down the street at a wild gallop, scattering pedestrians, dogs, pigs, and pigeons before them.

"Aieeeee!" Seamus cried, holding on to his hat with one hand and the dash rail of the coach with the other.

James kept his gaze trained on the street ahead as he wielded whip and reins skillfully, keeping the horses at their breakneck pace while doing his best to steer around other vehicles and obstacles in their path. Several times he heard gasps from Seamus or Sally, who was peering through the open window behind the driver's bench, as the coach narrowly missed hitting a parked carriage or running down a bystander, not to mention a time or two when it rounded a corner on two wheels. But each time James kept his focus, calling upon a lifetime of experience and steady hands to steer them through. Fortunately, the traffic was fairly light overall, and within a few minutes Mr. Chandler and the others were far behind them, lost to sight. Only then did James ease the team back into a brisk trot and check on the others.

"Everyone all right?" he asked.

Beside him, Seamus was staring at him in wonder, clutching the edge of the seat with white-knuckled hands. "Sakes alive!" Seamus exclaimed breathlessly. "I didn't know you could drive like that!"

Sally popped her head through the window. "Indeed," she said. "I thought you'd gone mad, running away like that. I was certain Father would catch us."

James noticed that her voice was higher in pitch now than it had been at their first meeting back in Washington. He guessed she had been purposely deepening it when she spoke, in order to help maintain her disguise.

Seamus must not have noticed, however. He turned toward her. "Hey," he said. "What's all this with that fellow calling you Sally, anyway? I thought your name was Sam. What's going on?"

Sally smiled ruefully. Reaching up, she removed her hat and shook her head. Cascades of honey-blond hair fell down around her slim shoulders.

"That Mr. Morgan of yours isn't the only one who's ever gone missing in the world," she said. "When I heard Father meant to force me into marrying that ridiculous fool, Winston, I decided it might be best for me to disappear, too. And unfair as it is, it's a lot easier for a man to make his way alone in this world than it is for a woman. So I became Sam."

Seamus looked astonished, and James turned away to hide a grin. Even with all his conspiracy theories, it seemed Seamus could still be surprised!

His smile faded quickly as he realized that he had no idea what to do next. Here they were, driving along getting better acquainted as if they didn't have a care in the world. But that was hardly the case.

"Listen," he said, interrupting Sally's additional explanations to Seamus about her situation. "We can talk about all that later. Right now, we need to decide what to do next."

Sally met his eye, a hint of suspicion evident in her expression. "As I see it, what we do next depends somewhat on what you've done up until now," she said. "Were you the ones who told Father where he might find me? Was that meeting a setup?"

"Not us!" Seamus interjected quickly. "We would never do such a thing, would we, James?"

James winced. "Er . . ." At Seamus's startled glance, he shrugged. "I saw her picture on a flyer—there was a reward. . . ."

"Just as I thought." Sally scowled at him. "Perhaps I'd better disembark right here, then. I wouldn't want you to be tempted to change your mind again should Father happen to increase the price upon my head, as well he could—he is one of the richest men in Baltimore, you know."

"Don't be a fool," James said, a bit stung by her words and the distrust in her eyes. "I obviously thought better of my actions, didn't I? Else we should not be here now."

Both of the others were staring at him, unconvinced. But there was no time to worry about that. Even if they had forgotten that they were most likely still being pursued, he had not.

"Here's a thought," James said, quickly formulating a plan. "We immediately head straight out of town. As soon as we're a good distance away, we drop Sally at some conveniently located hack stable, where she can hire a horse to take her to Washington or perhaps some city even farther away—Philadelphia, Williamsburg, or elsewhere—where she can disappear again into her identity as Sam."

"And what about you two?" Sally asked.

James shrugged, flicking the reins to steer around a hole in the street. "We return home."

She shook her head. "That won't do. What of my father?"

"Oh, I'll return the money he already gave me, of course." James winced, already missing the cash but glad he'd spent little of it so far. "That should take care of him."

"Don't be so certain."

"Well, then I'll speak with my father about how to handle him," James said. "Or my brother Thomas, or perhaps even my brother-in-law, Arthur, will be of some use to me, for once—he is accustomed to dealing with surly customers and such, I am sure."

"No, you don't understand." Sally leaned forward again until half of her body was hanging out over the driver's seat between James and Seamus, the latter of whom still seemed stunned enough to be keeping quiet for once. "My father didn't become one of the wealthiest men in Baltimore by giving up easily once he'd set his mind to something. And he most definitely is a person who can hold a grudge. He won't be talked out of punishing you for this. Not by your father or brother, not by anyone."

James felt a chill go down his spine at her words. Meanwhile, Seamus blinked, jabbing his finger toward a turnoff they'd just passed.

"Hey," he said. "If we're leaving town to head home, you should have gone back that way, shouldn't you?"

James realized Seamus was right. He also realized that

he'd automatically been steering the coach in the direction of the address Mr. Meriwether Clark had given them. Even though he'd all but forgotten about Mr. Clark in the excitement of the past few minutes, some part of his mind had retained the plan of the day and was carrying it out.

And that suddenly gave him a new idea. "Perhaps Sally is right," he said. "Perhaps we shouldn't try to return home after all. It might be better to get away for a while, allow things to blow over."

"What do you mean?" Seamus glanced nervously back over one shoulder as if expecting Mr. Chandler to overtake them at any moment.

The coach took the next corner with the horses still at a trot. Half a block ahead, James could see a man standing at the edge of the street in front of a respectable-looking boardinghouse. Beside him was a small heap of trunks and boxes, and it appeared he had just pulled out a pocketwatch to check the time.

James smiled. "Look, Mr. Clark is ready and waiting."

For a moment Seamus looked confused. Then a grin spread across Seamus's narrow face. "Oh, I see," he said, some of the usual lightheartedness returning to his voice. "Well, we shouldn't keep him waiting any longer, I suppose." He let out a chuckle.

"What?" Sally looked from one of them to the other, her expression confused and a bit annoyed. "What are you on about? This is no laughing matter, you know."

"Indeed." James glanced at her. "Perhaps you should put your hat back on. We're going to pick up a passenger now."

"What? A passenger! I repeat—what are you on about? Are you mad? My father—"

But there was no time for further explanations. As long as they remained in the city, it would be easy enough for Sally's father to track them down. If he had hired a fast phaeton or curricle as quickly as possible once they'd careened out of sight, he could already be catching up to them at that very moment. If James's new plan was to work, they had to hurry. He would fill Sally in later, once they were out of town.

James brought the team to an abrupt halt in front of the waiting Mr. Clark. "Good morning, sir," he said, swinging down from the driver's seat. "Sorry we're a bit tardy."

Seamus had leaped down just as quickly and was already

gathering up as much of the luggage as he could hold at one time. "Not to worry, sir," he said breathlessly, staggering toward the coach door. "We'll be on the road before you know it."

"Don't hurry on my account," Mr. Clark said, glancing at the sweaty team, now chomping and foaming upon their bits as they stood with heads down and flanks heaving. "It's a long trip ahead of us. A few minutes here or there won't make much difference. If you'd like to rest your horses before we depart—"

"Sooner started, sooner finished," James said briskly, trying to sound efficient rather than panicky. Resisting the urge to peer down the street for any sign of pursuit, he instead grabbed the largest trunk and yanked it along toward the coach door. "Come along, sir, let's get you comfortable in the back. I hope you won't mind sharing the journey with our friend, er, Sam."

"Not at all." Mr. Clark tipped his hat in Sally's direction as he climbed into the coach. She had hastily tucked her hair back under her cap and looked as much a boy as she ever had.

Meanwhile, Seamus was helping James hoist the trunk

into the body of the coach. "There we are," he said, tossing a few smaller items of luggage in after the trunk and then swinging himself back into the passenger seat as nimbly as a monkey. "Let's be off!"

James closed the coach door on the still surprised-looking Mr. Clark. Seconds later he was behind the team again urging them back into a trot. He knew the horses were tired, but they were fit enough to maintain the faster pace a bit longer. They could rest and walk a while once they were safely out of the city.

He glanced over at Seamus, who had seemingly recovered fully from his confusion and worry and now had a delighted gleam in his eyes. Could he actually be enjoying this crazy ride? James was perplexed as always by Seamus's odd nature. Still, he appreciated the way he was playing along without even knowing exactly what James had in mind to do next.

It's the same way he and Sally both came along without pause or protest when I ran away from Mr. Chandler back in the square, he told himself with some wonder. *I don't know why they trusted me so instantly. I'm not at all sure I could do the same if our situations were reversed.*

Deciding not to worry about that, he clenched the reins and whip more tightly in his hands. Mr. Clark was right— they had a long journey ahead of them. For now, he needed to focus long enough to get them safely out of Baltimore, or it would be over before it began. Glancing up just long enough to determine the position of the sun, he thereafter took the first opportunity to turn the coach due west.

Seven

"Is he asleep?" James asked, glancing back from the driver's seat.

Seamus turned and peered back into the body of the coach at Mr. Clark. The older man was on the rear seat leaning into the corner, his feet propped up on his trunk. He was perfectly still, seeming little bothered by the occasional jouncing and jarring of the coach. They were about a week's journey out of Baltimore by now, traveling through the state of Ohio upon the relatively smooth macadam of the Cumberland Road. Also known as the National Road, it stretched all the way from Maryland to Illinois. James had just steered them carefully past a small herd of cattle on their way to market and was now settled in comfortably behind a public stagecoach.

Sally was seated at the other end of the rear seat. "Mr. Clark, are you awake?" she inquired in a quiet tone. When the man did not stir, she looked up toward James and

Seamus and nodded. "He's asleep. We can talk."

She crawled forward, being careful not to kick Mr. Clark in the confined space. Soon she was wriggling through the opening between the driver's seat and the back. James looked over in surprise as she settled herself in the small area of bench between him and Seamus.

"What?" she demanded at his look, smoothing out the legs of her pants.

"Nothing," James said. "It's just that I wouldn't have expected you to climb up here that way."

"You wouldn't seem so surprised if I were truly a boy rather than merely dressed as one, would you?" Sally retorted.

She had maintained her disguise throughout the journey so far, none of them wanting to explain to their passenger or anyone else they might encounter why an unescorted young lady was traveling with them. However, Sally was careful always to procure herself her own room at the roadside inns where they spent their nights, generally waiting until Mr. Clark had disappeared into his room before speaking with the clerk. Luckily, she had a little money with her, and along with the sum her father had given James and the meager stipend Arthur had allowed James and Seamus for the trip, they were all able to afford decent lodgings and food along the way.

"Er, true enough, I suppose," James stammered in response to her comment, once again a bit taken aback by her directness. She had repeatedly surprised him this past week. Although not what most would consider ladylike, Sally's plain manner of speaking did carry a certain charm. "But never mind. Let us not waste the opportunity to talk while Mr. Clark is asleep."

Over the course of the journey so far, the three of them had discovered that Mr. Clark was a very deep sleeper, and made a loud and distinctive grumble and snort upon coming awake. Once he had dozed off, as he did several times per day, they could talk openly in their normal tones of voice without fearing that he would overhear a word. In that way, they had managed to keep their current predicament from him thus far.

However, despite discussing it at every opportunity, they had not yet determined exactly what to do next. For the moment, James was trying only to put as much distance as possible between themselves and Baltimore.

Early on, they all had debated the possibility of taking a different, less-traveled route in case Sally's father should somehow figure out where they were headed and decide to pursue. But despite the arguments of the other two in favor of this plan, James ultimately had decided that it was not worth the extra risk, and that they would remain on the well-traveled Cumberland Road all the way through to Vandalia, Illinois. After all, what would they do if an axle broke or a horse went lame on some more obscure passage? It was not yet winter, but the nights were already growing cooler, plus James didn't like to imagine what Arthur would say if he returned a coach damaged by overly rough roads. Adding weight to the decision was their passenger. They would have to come up with some sort of explanation for Mr. Clark, who had made this journey a number of times before and would surely notice if they departed from the usual route. Seamus tried to suggest that they convince him they were only doing it to avoid making him pay the tolls of the National Pike, but James was quick to point out that to a man of Mr. Clark's means, financial savings certainly would not seem a fair trade for a much longer and more arduous journey.

"Did you hear what Clark had to say earlier today about what is truly involved in becoming a third-degree Freemason?" Seamus asked eagerly, shooting another glance at the sleeping passenger. His eyes were gleaming with excitement when he looked back at James. "With a bit more time, I can get him to share some real secrets of the order, I warrant!"

James rolled his eyes. Seamus had been questioning their passenger at every opportunity about his father's involvement with the Masons and similar topics. Mr. Clark had responded to his queries with unfailing good cheer, which Seamus seemed to take as encouragement to continue with ever more probing questions. For his part, James suspected that the older man knew very well what his interviewer was about. Seamus was not nearly so clever with his interrogation as he thought he was.

"Forget your Freemason mystery," he said. "It won't be long before we're in St. Louis, and then we shall have to make some decisions. What are we going to do about Sally's father?"

The longer this trip continued, the more anxious James was feeling about the future, to the point where he was having trouble sleeping at night and his stomach was in knots at all times. If only he'd never seen that flyer! If only he'd thought better of responding to it—resisted the lure of easy money and turned away without giving it further thought. Why hadn't he minded his own business as he normally did? James felt as if he'd ruined not only his own life, but the lives of Sally and Seamus as well. How could this have happened?

It doesn't seem fair, he thought for the umpteenth time over the past few days. *All this time I've been the quiet one in the family, the responsible one. I don't run off after imagined treasure all the time, like Father and Thomas. I don't roughhouse like Will and Sam and Arthur. I don't even gossip like Eleanor. So how is it that I am now the one on the run and not knowing what to do?*

"What about the idea I mentioned before?" Sally spoke up, jarring James out of his gloomy thoughts. "Once we've left Mr. Clark at his destination, why don't we just keep going? We could disappear, start a new life somewhere in the West. . . ."

James sighed. They'd been over this many times already. He had mostly kept quiet on the subject, as Sally and Seamus seemed content to argue it out between themselves.

Seamus seemed somewhat tempted by the possibility of investigating the disappearance of Mr. Morgan out West, where he was said by some to be hiding to that day—not to mention the hope of making it all the way to California, where they might find their share of that recently discovered gold. On the other hand, now that he was being presented with the hard, cold reality of such dreamy plans, he was clearly growing reluctant to leave his father behind for such an extended period of time.

"I am all that my father has since my mother died and my older sister married and moved out," he said whenever the subject arose. "He is expecting me home again in New York as soon as the worst of the epidemic has passed. He would be heartbroken without me."

Each time he said it, James felt a mixture of relief and disappointment. There was something tantalizing in the idea of leaving his old life behind and continuing on into the unknown, untamed West. Was that not exactly what he'd daydreamed about many times before—starting over? True, his daydreams had not usually included embracing a life of certain hardship beyond the Western frontier. But he was accustomed to hard labor from his work in the stable, and it was said by many that there was no better place for a man to make his fortune than the Mexican Cession and other new territory to the west. Besides, there was no law saying he could not return one day after Mr. Chandler's anger had blown over. . . .

"No," he blurted out, arguing against himself as much as against Sally. "I have told you before, it is foolish even to speak of it." He grimaced, hating that he sounded like such a killjoy. "For one thing, it would turn us into horse thieves. As soon as the coach went missing, Arthur would have us tracked down and hanged."

Seamus let out a snort. "True enough, he most probably would," he agreed. "Anyone fancy a bite to eat?" he then asked, patting his stomach. "I think there is some salt pork in one of the bags."

He clambered back into the body of the coach. Mr. Clark was still sleeping and did not stir as Seamus dug into the bags and boxes near his feet.

"Find anything?" Sally asked, watching him. "I might have a bite if you do."

"No, but look at this!" Seamus said after a moment, sounding surprised. He pulled a bundle from beneath one of Mr. Clark's boxes. "We forgot to drop off the mail."

"What mail?" Sally asked.

James quickly explained about the bundle of mail they'd picked up at the tavern just before meeting her. "I hope there was nothing urgent there," he commented. "But I suppose this gives us all the more reason to return home as soon as we figure out how to handle Mr. Chandler."

Seamus flopped down on the seat, flipping through the letters and packages. "I haven't had a letter from my father in a while," he said. "Perhaps there is something from him in this batch. That would be a fortuitous surprise, would it not?"

"A surprise indeed." James's mind was already wandering back to their dilemma. What were they to do? If what Sally said was true, Mr. Chandler would be upon them the moment they returned to the East Coast. He could return the reward money and offer to work off the paltry amount he'd already spent. But he suspected that would not make up for throwing the spoiled milk in his face—nor for spiriting his daughter away again just when he'd had her within his grasp.

Before he could reach any new conclusions, Seamus let

out a cry of surprise. "Look here!" he exclaimed, pulling one letter from the bundle of mail. "It's addressed to your father, James—and the sender is Eleanor Gates Darby!"

"Aunt Ellie!" James took both reins in one hand and twisted around. "Give it here—let's see if she writes anything about that so-called treasure. Perhaps now that the news of that gold discovery is out, she will feel comfortable giving more specific news if that is what she was on about before."

He felt no small measure of guilt as he opened the letter, knowing it had been intended for his father's eyes, not his. But he squashed the feeling as best he could. He had far bigger things to be remorseful about.

Aunt Ellie's neat, loopy handwriting looked the same as always. The letter began with the usual chatty news about her children and grandchildren. Before James could get any farther than that, Seamus let out another cry.

"I knew it!" he cried, waving another letter he'd just found in the stack. "It's for me, from New York." He peered at the outside, looking a bit puzzled. "Oh. But it is not from Father after all. It's from my sister, Brigid."

James knew little of Seamus's older sister except that she

had married several years earlier and now had three or four children of her own. As far as he knew, she had not written to Seamus since his arrival in Maryland, though letters had come from Franklin nearly once a week.

Turning his gaze back to the letter in his own hand, James scanned through another paragraph of his aunt's news. There came the sound of rustling paper from where Seamus was sitting, then silence. James glanced back after a moment and saw that Seamus's face had crumpled as he stared down at the letter from his sister.

"What is it?" James asked, alarmed.

James's comment caused Sally to turn around, too. "Seamus?" she asked, sounding instantly concerned. When Seamus did not answer or even look up, she crawled back into the coach to sit beside him. "What is the matter? Is it bad news?"

"The worst." Seamus finally looked up and met their eyes. A single tear squeezed from his eye and made a track down his cheek. "It—it is my father."

"What of him? Is he ill?" James asked.

"Worse than that." Seamus gulped. "He is gone. Cholera. The epidemic has—has taken him."

At Seamus's words, Sally let out a gasp of shock. For his part, James felt his whole person go hot and then cold, and he had no idea what to say. Though he had never had the chance to meet Franklin Poole, nor even seen a picture of him, spending so much time with Seamus these past several months had made him feel as if it were a family member who had just been reported dead.

Seamus was staring down at the letter again, the tears coming faster now. Sally bit her lip and glanced at James. He stared back, not wanting to look any longer at Seamus's bleak little face. Nobody spoke for a moment, and the only sounds were the rumble of the coach wheels, the steady breathing of the horses, and Mr. Clark's snoring.

"I'm sorry, Seamus," Sally said at last, her tone subdued. She put a hand on his arm. "I'm so very, very sorry."

"And me," James added, swallowing hard. "I know—I know your father was always good to you. He sounds like he is—was—er, a fine man."

Seamus didn't respond or move. For a moment James wasn't sure if he'd even heard them.

Then he finally looked up. "This settles it, I suppose," he said in an odd, strangled voice very unlike his usual happy-go-lucky tone. "There is nothing for me in the East anymore." Glancing at Sally, he swiped the tears from his face and jutted his narrow chin forward with determination. "If you are sincere in wanting to continue west from St. Louis, I am with you."

Eight

James had no intention of arguing against Seamus's new determination while the shock of his father's death was still fresh. And by the time another day had passed, his impulse to do so at all was fading. After all, were his own feelings really so different? What was there for him to return to at home? A miserable life answering to Arthur as his own aging father and distant brother drifted even further off into their own treasure-hunting fantasy world?

True, the alternative plan was not so certain as he might have liked. There was no telling whether they could make it all the way to California, or find gold or any other means of support there if they did. As for Aunt Ellie's letters, it seemed even more open to question that her so-called clues—including one more in the latest letter—were truly leading to anything profitable. But what if they were? His father appeared to have passed up the chance to find out, mesmerized as he was by his dreams of Charlotte. Would

James be making the same mistake by turning back now? Was he not willing to take any risk in pursuit of his own, much more practical dreams?

The long, dull journey gave him plenty of time to ponder such matters. As the macadam passed beneath the coach's wheels, mile by mile through Ohio and then Indiana, James began to see the benefits of Sally's plan. What did he have to lose? If he struck it rich out west in one way or another, he could then return home in triumph, knowing that Arthur and his ilk no longer had any dominion over him. If not, then what point in returning at all, only to be pushed off into the corner again? Surely he could work at some menial job in the West just as well as he could at home, if required. At least that way he would finally be his own man.

One day, midway across Indiana, the travelers stopped at a roadside inn for some refreshment. They walked in and immediately noted a noisy commotion at the back of the dining area. There had to be at least a dozen people gathered there already, and still more were flowing from all directions to join it like tributaries rushing into a river.

"I wonder what is going on over there?" Mr. Clark commented, following them inside.

Seamus shrugged, seeming little interested. He had been glum and quiet, keeping mostly to himself since receiving the news about his father. James never would have thought he would miss Seamus's incessant chatter and nearly inexhaustible energy. But now he found himself longing to see him laugh or hear him ask Mr. Clark another in his endless supply of queries about the inner workings of the Freemasons.

Sally stood on her tiptoes and craned her neck to see. "A group of people are gathered around a fellow at one of the tables over there," she reported. "Come, let us see who he might be."

For his part, James would have preferred to sit down immediately and rest. He was well used to driving or riding nearly every day, but being on the road for so long at a stretch was surprisingly wearing on both mind and body. Still, he trailed along as the others hurried across the room to satisfy their curiosity.

"Sakes alive," Mr. Clark exclaimed mildly as they drew closer and had a view of the man at the center of the ruckus. "I do believe that is Mr. Kit Carson."

"Kit Carson?" Seamus wrinkled his nose and shook his head as he surveyed the man in the center of the throng.

"That skinny little fellow? With all due respect, sir, I think you must be mistaken."

James had to agree. Like everyone, he had read of the exploits of Kit Carson—the rough and tumble mountain man, the skilled wilderness guide who had helped John C. Frémont's expeditions survive harsh terrain and native attacks in the far West, the brave fighter who had served in the recently ended war against Mexico. The man sitting before them now looked nothing like the mythic figure he had imagined was behind all that. About forty years of age, with a freckled face, this fellow was as short and slight of stature as Seamus, with stooped shoulders, light reddish hair, and gentle blue eyes.

"No, I am quite certain," Mr. Clark insisted. "I met him once before when he was on his way through St. Louis carrying a message to Washington."

Seamus still looked dubious, but Clark was already pushing his way forward through the crowds surrounding the man. He was soon shaking hands with Carson, and from what James could see, managed to exchange a few words with the great hero before being shuffled back by others eagerly desiring to make Carson's acquaintance.

By the time Clark returned to their little group, Seamus had perked up with interest. "So that is truly him, then?" he demanded. "The famous Kit Carson? I must go and meet him as well!"

He rushed forward with Sally at his heels. James hung back with Mr. Clark, feeling a bit shy of pressing himself upon the great man. "He looks nothing like I might have expected," he mused aloud, staring as Seamus eagerly shook Carson's hand. "After hearing of all his exploits out west, I thought he would be seven feet tall and broad as an ox."

"True enough," Clark agreed. "Then again, the truth of a man's character and accomplishments does not always match up perfectly with what people expect of him. Nor does his appearance necessarily belie his abilities. And it is certain that Kit Carson is a man of tremendous accomplishment, despite how he may appear." He smiled and patted his belly. "Now come, James—let us find a seat and then some hearty grub. I am famished."

Seamus and Sally soon returned, bubbling over with the excitement of having met a man of such celebrity. They had learned that Carson was on his way back west after a brief visit to Washington.

"Probably delivering some important message about the gold discovery to President Polk," Seamus guessed as he stood by the table James and Mr. Clark had procured. His eyes were showing more of their usual sparkle for the first time since they had fallen upon that fateful letter. "I wonder what it said?"

Sally laughed. "I'm surprised you didn't ask," she teased. "Have you suddenly gone shy, Seamus?"

"Shy? No. Hmm . . ." Seamus glanced back toward Carson, once again nearly hidden from them by admirers, as if considering heading over there again to ask. Sally dragged him into a seat and playfully ordered him to stay put.

By the time they finished eating, Mr. Carson had departed—and the crowds of admirers along with him. But Sally, Seamus, and even Mr. Clark spent the rest of that day's ride excitedly recounting all Mr. Carson's exploits that they could remember. James listened as he drove, glad to see Seamus acting a bit more in character, but he added little to the discussion himself. As he heard Mr. Clark vividly describe a bloody battle against the Klamath Lake natives of the Oregon Territory, James found himself wondering uneasily what he would do were he to encounter such hostile natives himself. So far, the idea of heading west had seemed mostly fun—albeit necessary—adventure. But now that the final decision on what to do loomed closer with every passing day, James found himself lingering more often over the nitty-gritty details of the proposed journey. They would be making their own way across untamed lands with no idea what to expect—and no Kit Carson to guide them or fight their battles if necessary.

Could they do it? James wasn't sure. At least he had grown up in the country—he was accustomed to dealing with dangerous animals, the vagaries of severe weather, and other manner of ordinary ills they might encounter along the way. But what of city-raised Seamus? Would he be able to handle even that much? Then there was Sally. James hardly counted against her anymore the fact that she was female, for she was proving herself the equal of any of them in almost every way. However, she too had been born and raised in the city. What skills did their motley crew truly have for surviving and thriving on the frontier?

The next day was dull and dreary, the iron gray clouds hinting at the fast approaching winter. There was little to see out the sides of the coach other than the other carriages and riders on the road and the constant line of inns, blacksmith shops, and livery stables along the way. Mr. Clark dropped off to sleep within the first hour, giving the others a chance to talk.

Partly to distract himself from his continuing worries over the future and also hoping to keep Seamus from brooding too much over his grief, James broached the subject of Aunt Ellie's letters. "We still have not decided what that second clue means," he said, pulling the missive in question from his pocket. The road was straight and smooth, and for once they were not completely surrounded by other traffic, leaving him free to focus on something other than driving as the horses made their steady way along.

"As far as I can tell, we haven't decided about the first one, either," Seamus pointed out.

James shrugged. "I suppose that may be true," he said. "But from its wording, I strongly suspect that it is meant only to introduce the quest, as I've said before. A sort of invitation to the game, if that makes sense."

"It does to me," Sally said, leaning forward from the rear

compartment. "It might be different if your aunt were able to communicate with your father face-to-face. But as she must express herself only in writing from beginning to end, it is only logical that she should be extra careful to make herself as clear as possible while still not giving away any secrets to outside eyes."

"Yes." James glanced around to smile at her. The more he came to know Sally, the more amazing he found it that the two of them seemed to think so much alike in some ways—though in others, of course, the workings of her mind remained completely foreign to him. "So let's have a look at the second one and see if we can puzzle it out."

"All right," Seamus agreed. His mood was still nothing like it had been before. But bits of his usual cheer were already starting to shine through the gloom now and then, like stray sunbeams after a rain. "What's the verse again? I've forgotten."

"Let me see." Sally took the letter from James and read it aloud. "'*Where our joyful old friend had his last Stand, begin to Trace your journey out across the land.*'" She pursed her lips and looked up at the other two. "All right, what do you suppose that could mean?"

"Joyful old friend," James echoed thoughtfully. Recalling his earlier theory that the phrase might refer to Franklin Poole, he shot a glance at Seamus. Under the present circumstances, he didn't quite dare bring it up unless one of the others mentioned it first. "Who could she mean by that?" he queried instead. "Do you have any theories, Sally?"

"Isn't it obvious?" a voice spoke from the back of the coach. "It must be my namesake, Mr. Meriwether Lewis."

James gasped, nearly dropping the reins as he spun around. Mr. Clark had awakened without any of them noticing. And judging by his comment, he had heard every word of their conversation!

Nine

After a moment of stunned silence, all three of them began to talk at once. Each of them tried—not very successfully—to explain things to their passenger. For his part, James felt a mixture of guilt, worry, and relief. It had been difficult keeping their secrets from Mr. Clark all this time. It might be easier now that he knew.

Fortunately, Mr. Clark had inherited some of his father's adventurous spirit. Rather than being upset that they had tried to deceive him for so long, he seemed excited and ready to join in the task of deciphering the clues.

"What fun! A puzzle to occupy our minds for the rest of our long, dull journey. I only wish I'd caught you at it earlier—especially as I suspected something was afoot amongst the three of you almost from the first day," he said with a twinkle in his eyes. "Several times when I was just coming awake, I had the distinct sense that the three of you were whispering and staring at me." He raised an eyebrow at

Sally. "Although I must confess, until I heard James call you by your true name, I had not put two and two together and worked out that you were female. I did, however, think you by far the prettiest boy I'd ever met."

Seamus laughed, and Sally blushed a deep red. "Well then," she said, reaching up to remove her hat. "I suppose there's no need to wear this itchy old thing while we're on the road. You all will have to remind me to put it on before we stop, that's all." She shook out her hair, then reached back and expertly tied it into a loose chignon at the nape of her neck.

Mr. Clark smiled. "Now then," he said, rubbing his hands and looking around at them. "Shall we have a good crack at deciphering that clue of yours?"

"All right." James glanced at him. "Why did you say the verse had to refer to the late Mr. Lewis?"

"It was not the whole verse but rather the phrase 'our joyful old friend,'" Clark explained. "Joyful means much the same as merry—which brings to mind the given name I share with Mr. Lewis—Meriwether. And Seamus here has mentioned several times that his father was acquainted with my father and Mr. Lewis in the days of their great exploration, so I am assuming that your father and aunt would have known him as well."

"Wait. They did? I mean, he did?" James blinked, realizing that quite a bit of Seamus's incessant chatter must have passed through his ears without him really hearing it. "My father knew Lewis and Clark?"

"Of course!" Seamus looked over at him in surprise. "Has he not told you of those days? It was when they all ran away from home more than forty years ago and had their adventures out West in the days of the Louisiana Purchase. This was back when Mr. Clark's home of Missouri was not yet even a state."

James's head spun. His father had mentioned those days, though as far as James could recall he'd never included Lewis and Clark in the telling. At least not to him.

As difficult as it might be to imagine his father rubbing elbows with the famous explorers all those years ago, it was all starting to make sense. No wonder his father had been so quick to give in and agree to this journey as soon as he'd learned that the passenger was to be Mr. Clark's son. Adam Gates had never been the most practical of men, and that bit of nostalgia would almost certainly be enough to make him change his mind, whereas a different sort, like Arthur or Will, would not give it a second thought.

James rubbed his forehead with his free hand. "All right," he said weakly. "Let us assume that that theory is correct, then. What of the rest of the verse?"

"May I hear it once more?" Mr. Clark glanced at Sally.

She obliged, reading it aloud again. "'*Where our joyful old friend had his last Stand, begin to Trace your journey out across the land.*'"

"Stand," Clark echoed thoughtfully. "Last stand. There is something familiar about—" He slapped the edge of the coach and grinned. "I have it! It is quite a clever play on words, really. Your aunt must be an intelligent and discerning woman, James."

"But what does it mean?" Sally asked, sounding a bit impatient. "Have you figured it out?"

"I believe so." Mr. Clark smiled. "You see, the esteemed Mr. Lewis tragically met his demise at a tavern in Tennessee known as Grinder's Stand. That establishment is located on the now-abandoned roadway between Tennessee and Mississippi known as the Natchez Trace. Do you see? His last stand—Grinder's Stand. Trace your journey—Natchez Trace. Clever, eh?"

"Indeed," James said thoughtfully, taking up the reins in both hands as they approached a slow-moving drove of hogs in the road. But even as he steered carefully around the animals, his mind was turning over this new bit of information. "So what does that mean to us? Are we to follow the Natchez Trace? Is it even still passable?"

"But the Trace runs southward to Mississippi," Seamus pointed out. "From the phrasing it sounds as if we are meant to go *out*, which seems to me to mean west."

"Unless Ellie was being careless with her words," Sally put in.

Mr. Clark shook his head, silencing Sally's protest. "Judging by the rest, the author of this verse is anything but careless. She could be merely using the Stand as a sort of marker or way station, including Trace only to make it a little easier to figure. She may not mean for you to actually follow the Trace at all."

"I hope not," James said. "That would take us well out of our way. In fact, even making our way to this Grinder's Stand in Tennessee seems rather problematic, especially so late in the season."

"But we cannot just sit back and ignore it," Seamus

argued. "If this clue is leading us to Tennessee, then that is where we should go."

"But as Mr. Clark just said, we do not even know if that is what Aunt Ellie meant," Sally countered, holding tightly to the edge of the coach as it bounced over a rough spot in the road. "After all, she does say we should next go 'out' across the land. That seems to indicate that we should continue westward. And it seems of little consequence whether we head west from Natchez Trace or from St. Louis. It is all the same if the endpoint lies in California."

"But we do not know that it does," Seamus pointed out.

"Did your aunt send any additional clues, James?" Mr. Clark spoke up.

James nodded. "I have seven letters in total with similar verses in them," he said. "This one is second in the sequence."

"Well, shall we have a look at the third, then?" the man suggested. "Perhaps that will offer to illuminate the matter."

The others agreed, and because they were by now safely ahead of the hogs, James collected the reins in one hand. He then pulled out the next letter in the sequence—for even in his pocket, he kept them carefully in order according to date—and handed it to Sally.

"Here we are," she said, unfolding it and scanning down until she found the verse. She read it aloud.

> A prophet with a Vision
> for earthly as well as heavenly Crown;
> Chased from the Garden of Eden
> he founded a Beautiful new town.
> (Pass westerly through
> and await your next clue!)

"Hmm," Seamus said when she'd finished. "What do you suppose that means?"

Mr. Clark shook his head and for a moment, all was silent. "At first it seems gibberish, indeed," he finally said. "But I am certain it holds meaning if we can only decipher it. Let's take it piece by piece and see if we can make sense of it. 'A prophet with a vision . . .'"

"Prophet," Sally mused aloud. "Prophet. That could refer to many things or people. However, the first that comes to my mind is—"

"Joseph Smith, Jr.!" Seamus finished for her, his eyes flashing eagerly. "That was the first thought to my mind, as well. What other prophet has been so talked about these past ten or twenty years, after all?"

James recalled that the two of them had mentioned the founder of the Mormon religion fairly regularly in the course of discussing the mystery of William Morgan. "Hold on a moment," he said. "Isn't that the fellow you say married that Morgan fellow's widow or some such? What does that nonsense have to do with this?"

"Married a widow?" Mr. Clark looked a bit confused. "I know nothing of that. But I think you two could be correct regarding the late Mr. Smith. He was seen by his followers as a prophet, and his various alleged visions are well documented."

"Yes." Sally shot James a condescending glance. "That is what I was thinking of indeed."

James felt a bit foolish, and found himself wishing he paid more attention to current events—and his friends. He vowed to do so from now on. "Smith was killed a few years back, was he not?" he asked.

"He was. And it happened not far from where we are

right now," Sally said with a nod. "In Carthage, near his home of Nauvoo, in the very state of Illinois through which we are currently traveling." Perhaps taking notice of James's rather confused expression, she added, "Nauvoo is where Smith and his followers fled after being chased out of Missouri."

"And Nauvoo itself seems to be part of our clue," Mr. Clark said. "If I am not mistaken, the town's name means something like 'beautiful place' or 'beautiful city.'"

"'A beautiful new town!'" Seamus quoted with a grin. "Well done, Mr. Clark!"

"But what of the second and third lines?" James asked. He was still trying to keep up with the whole conversation. "The bit about 'heavenly Crown' makes sense, as it seems to be referring to a religious prophet. But what is the significance of the earthly crown? Or the Garden of Eden, for that matter?"

"I know!" Seamus exclaimed. "The part about the earthly crown, anyway. I have read that in his younger days Mr. Smith was a treasure hunter."

James grimaced. Could he never get away from treasure hunting? Not only did it seem he was on one of his own, but now even the clues were about hunts. "Is that so?" he said. "Well then I suppose it does make sense. I know from personal experience that that particular breed sees their quest as nearly a religious pursuit, to the point that they spend the largest part of their energy striving for earthly crowns, not to mention earthly gold, earthly jewels . . ."

Mr. Clark shot him a curious glance, perhaps startled by James's suddenly bitter tone. But he did not ask any questions. Instead he leaned past Sally and pointed to the third line of verse.

"If I am not mistaken, one of Mr. Smith's beliefs was that the historical Garden of Eden actually lies in Jackson County, Missouri. And as Miss Chandler just mentioned, it was from Missouri that he and his followers were chased by the Extermination Order of the Governor about ten years back."

"So that's it, then!" Seamus laughed aloud, perhaps for the first time since receiving the letter from his sister. "We've solved the whole thing."

"Have we?" James shrugged. "But what is it telling us? Merely to keep on through Nauvoo to the West? That is not particularly enlightening."

"All right," Sally agreed. "But at least now we may feel confident in not turning south to follow the Natchez Trace, which appears to have been merely a further clue to the first verse after all, not a direction itself."

James had to admit that was true enough. Still, he was becoming more uneasy about this whole adventure. Once again he found himself thinking of the stories he'd heard of the games, codes, and puzzles that his father and aunt were said to have enjoyed teasing each other with in their youth—all for nothing but entertainment. Was there actually something tangible at the end of the trail, or was Aunt Ellie merely leading them on some playful wild-goose chase? Is that why his father had not bothered to follow the clues himself?

Seamus and Sally obviously had no such worries. They were already discussing the logistics of following the clue through Nauvoo to the West once they'd dropped off Mr. Clark—could they make it to California if they left now, or would it be safer to wait until spring to tackle the arduous journey? For his part, Mr. Clark seemed eager to see the next letter.

"This clue has already given us a hint as to your next

move," he pointed out. "If all goes well, we should be in St. Louis sometime tomorrow. Before then, perhaps I can help decipher the rest of the clues and steer you more steadily on your way."

James glanced at him, amazed at the way the man had thrown himself wholeheartedly into this pursuit. He seemed to have accepted their quest at face value without even wondering at the idea that they made no mention of returning to Baltimore. Did he not think that odd?

Or perhaps people in the West really do think differently than those back home, James thought. *After all, it surely takes a special type of individual to try to make a life out here, where nothing is guaranteed and death can come at any moment in a hundred different ways. Perhaps those types of people do not worry as much as the rest of us about such minor matters as propriety and predictability.*

"Where is the next letter, James?" Sally asked, poking him in the shoulder from her seat in the rear section of the coach. "Hand it back here so that Mr. Clark might have a look."

"All right, just a moment," James said, reaching into his pocket once more. "I have it right—"

"Halt!" a commanding voice shouted at that moment from somewhere just to the rear of the coach. "We have come for Miss Sally Chandler. If you wish to avoid trouble, stop and hand her over immediately!"

Sally gasped, turning and peering out the side. "It's Winston!" she cried. "He's found us!"

Ten

James glanced back and blanched. Sure enough, a familiar-looking, thin, sallow-faced figure was riding up behind them on a sweat-soaked gray horse. The large, silent, swarthy man who had been with Sally's father at the earlier confrontation was just behind Winston on a sturdy chestnut, and beside him rode a second stranger, burlier and meaner-looking than the other.

"How did they find us?" Seamus cried in alarm. "It's been nearly a fortnight since we left Baltimore!"

Mr. Clark looked confused. "What is happening?" he demanded. "Who are those men, and what do they want with you, Sally?"

"The one on the gray wants to marry me," she responded grimly. "And while this does not match at all with my own desires, he and my father seem not to care overmuch about that."

"I see," Mr. Clark replied, although his expression did not look convinced.

Meanwhile James slumped in the driver's seat, his fingers numb on the reins, feeling helpless. He glanced to the side of the road, trying to ascertain whether it was safe to pull over at this particular spot. After all, what other choice did they have but to obey Winston's command? There was no way their cumbersome coach could outrun three men on horseback, even if they were to try. In any case, that was not really an option—James could not in good conscience endanger Mr. Clark, who was no party to this situation. . . .

"Move aside, James," Mr. Clark said, climbing forward onto the driver's bench.

James blinked at him in surprise, not understanding for a moment. "What?" he said.

"Give me the reins." Mr. Clark took them from James's unresisting hands without awaiting a response. "I had better do the driving for now."

"But the coach—they are so much faster—we cannot—" James stammered uncertainly.

Mr. Clark shoved him bodily aside on the driver's bench, causing him in turn to nearly send Seamus tumbling off over the side. Seamus grabbed hold of a part of the coach just in time and clung to it, pushing himself back onto the edge of the bench.

"Hold on, everybody!" Mr. Clark shouted as he cracked the whip over the horses' backs. "This could be a wild ride."

The horses sprang forward at a gallop. Winston—or perhaps one of his companions—let out an angry shout from just behind them.

James looked back as the coach swayed wildly. Had Mr. Clark gone mad? Despite the advantage of surprise, the men's horses were scrabbling forward into a gallop even now. The gray was already rapidly closing the gap between itself and the coach.

"Oh, dear! Please, do not endanger yourselves!" Sally cried, holding tightly to the back of the driver's bench as the coach swayed and creaked. "We cannot possibly outrun them!"

"Do not be so certain, young lady." Mr. Clark smiled grimly. "Now grab hold—here we go!"

The coach suddenly careened hard to the left. For a second James feared that Mr. Clark meant to crash them straight into the trees that thickly lined this stretch of the road. However, he saw that the man had actually steered them onto a narrow, barely visible turnoff. James gasped, grabbing the dash rail with both hands to avoid being bounced out of his seat as the wheels left the smooth macadam and met the rough, rutted clay of the side road.

"They missed it! They went right on past the turn!" Seamus cheered. He was still crowded on the edge of the seat and hanging on to the side of the coach for dear life. This precarious position allowed him to lean over for a clear view behind them, though James feared Seamus might lose his grip and go flying off to the side at any moment, if he were not first smacked loose by a branch of one of the trees that lined either side of the narrow dirt road.

"It won't take them long to turn around and follow, though," Sally said. "It might be best to stop now and let me out, as there is little chance we can outrun them. They have the obvious advantage, being able to ride much faster than we can possibly drive."

"Don't worry, Miss Chandler," Mr. Clark said with a grin. "Their mounts may be nimbler, but they do not know these roads and trails as I do. For example, I doubt they shall even notice *this* one. . . ."

With that, he once again turned the carriage sharply,

this time to the right. They all ducked as several drooping pine branches swept over the front of the coach, smacking the trio on the driver's bench about the face and head and nearly removing James's cap. He brushed a pinecone out of his hair and winced as the coach tipped on the uneven trail, the two right wheels leaving the ground entirely.

"Lean left!" he shouted, throwing himself against Mr. Clark. The others immediately tossed their weight that way as well, and the coach once again settled onto all four wheels and rattled down the new road.

"Good thinking, James." Mr. Clark shot him a brief, admiring glance before returning his attention to the path ahead, which seemed little more than a deer track through the forest. "It's always good to share this sort of adventure with someone who can keep his wits about him."

James couldn't help feeling flattered by the compliment. But he didn't have time to luxuriate in the feeling. Blanching, he spotted a deep hole in the center of the trail. "Look out!" he shouted.

But Mr. Clark had already seen the hazard. Wielding the reins and whip skillfully, he immediately slowed the team and guided them safely past the hole.

"Nice driving, sir," James said with a sigh of relief. "I would have found that a challenge myself, particularly if I were driving an unfamiliar team."

Mr. Clark shot him another glance. "Thanks," he said. "But your fine team is hardly unfamiliar, after nearly two weeks spent gazing all day long at their hindquarters." He shrugged and smiled modestly. "In any case, I do like to fancy myself a fair horseman."

"Never mind that," Seamus broke in. "I want to know how in blazes those fellows found us?"

James had already figured out the answer. "Mr. Chandler knew my name and address from when I contacted him about, um . . ." He shot a glance at Sally, letting his voice trail off. "Anyway, he must have gotten in touch with Father or Arthur and found out where we were headed. With that information, it was a simple matter to ride after us."

Seamus blinked. "But would your family really give us away?" he exclaimed. "Even Arthur can't be quite so rotten, can he?"

"Oh, they probably didn't even realize they were doing it," Sally put in. "Father can be quite charming when he has need to be. I am quite certain he gave your relations no cause to suspect he meant you harm."

"Hmm. So these scoundrels have pursued you from Baltimore and may have known you were heading to St. Louis?" Mr. Clark said. "Well, it was indeed a simple matter to track you, then. There are not many likely routes between the one city and the other. All they had to do was ride fast enough to catch up."

"So what are we to do now? Surely they'll double back and find this turnoff soon enough." Seamus grimaced. "I knew we should have taken some other route, rather than waltzing down the National Road where anyone might find us as they pleased!"

"That would not have helped," James pointed out. "True, taking the well-traveled road allowed our pursuers to find us most easily. But any alternate route would have taken us considerably longer, guaranteeing that they would reach St. Louis well before us."

Sally nodded, biting her lower lip. "And then, all they would have had to do was lie in wait for us when we dropped off Mr. Clark," she finished. "Yes, I should have known that Father would find a way to catch me again.

Perhaps it was foolish even to try to escape."

"There, there." Mr. Clark took one hand off the reins long enough to reach back and pat her on the hand. "I have some small influence in these parts and may be able to help. If we can reach St. Louis before your pursuers find us again, perhaps I can contact the authorities there and help you work something out."

"It's no use." Sally sounded bleak. "Father is an expert at convincing the authorities to see things his way. Besides, what authority would refuse to return a rebellious daughter to her father, when we females are seen as little more than the property of men? No, all three of you have been more than kind to me. But I cannot endanger you any longer. It's time to turn myself over and end this." She sighed. "I'm sure being married to Winston shall not be nearly as horrible as I imagine."

"No!" James blurted out before he realized it. "Er, I mean, you cannot give up. We've come this far!"

Seamus nodded vigorously, nearly bouncing out of his seat again as the coach jounced over another rut. "Yes," he agreed. "Besides, James and I will never survive out West without you to keep us on the straight and narrow!"

Sally's responding smile looked rather wan. "True enough," she joked weakly.

Mr. Clark seemed thoughtful. "Fear not, all is not lost, my dear," he said. "I have another idea. We are only an hour or two east of Missouri by now. I know this area well. There is a settlement a few miles from here that we should be able to reach without going near the main road again. I can hire passage there to take me the rest of the way to St. Louis. Once you drop me off, perhaps you can stay ahead of your pursuers by taking some random direction. With care and a bit of luck, you could lose them and continue west as planned."

Sally lifted her head, a spark of hope lighting her eyes. "Do you truly think that could work?" she asked Clark. "But they are so close behind us now. . . ."

He nodded firmly. "Leave that part to me. I'll soon have them confounded."

Sally and Seamus both started talking at once, but James didn't respond. For one thing, he couldn't help feeling vaguely guilty about abandoning a paying passenger before reaching his destination, even if it was the passenger's own idea. Besides that, though, was there really any chance of throwing the pursuers off their trail long enough to put the plan into action? The coach was hardly inconspicuous, and though the ground was dry and rutted enough not to leave many obvious marks, they couldn't help but break branches and bring down flurries of brightly colored autumn leaves as they pushed their way down these little-traveled trails.

But he kept quiet about these worries, suspecting that the others would pay no mind anyway. Mr. Clark continued down the road a ways, then brought the team to a halt at an intersection with another, slightly larger and more traveled-looking dirt road.

"Why are you stopping?" Seamus cast an anxious glance behind them.

"Which of you has a hat or jacket to which you are not too attached?" Mr. Clark asked in response. "Hand it over, please."

Not really understanding what the request was about, James removed his well-worn hat and gave it to the man. Mr. Clark took it, nodded his thanks, and hopped down out of the coach. He stepped a few yards down the side trail, then tossed the hat onto the ground. On his way back to the coach, he reached up and yanked on a few of the lower-hanging branches, leaving them dangling half-broken behind him with their leaves scattered on the trail below.

"There," he said as he climbed back aboard, pausing just long enough to give the near-side horse a pat. "That should throw them off for a little while at least."

James nodded. Mr. Clark was laying a false trail in the hopes that their pursuers would go that way while they escaped in another direction. Perhaps they *did* have a chance after all.

"We shall have to find a place to stop for the night," Sally said, peering out of the coach into the quickly gathering dusk, which was even deeper beneath the shade of the tall trees surrounding them. "There's not much of a moon tonight, and besides, the horses can't go on much longer without a rest."

James chewed his lower lip, knowing she was right. As planned, they had left Mr. Clark at the inn in a tiny village several hours earlier. The town consisted of only a few houses in addition to the inn, and James had his doubts about how quickly the man would be able to find passage to

St. Louis. But as Mr. Clark didn't seem at all anxious about that, James had decided not to let it trouble him, either.

Since bidding farewell to Mr. Clark, James, Seamus, and Sally had been making their way along a succession of rough dirt roads, trying to continue more or less to the west, but putting a greater priority in staying clear of well-traveled roads or villages of any size. While Mr. Clark had been still with them, James had believed the plan could work. There had been a sense of security in the older man's knowledge and confidence. But now, with Mr. Clark gone, James's doubts were beginning to creep back again. Could they really do this?

"We could camp out for the night," Seamus suggested, breaking into James's thoughts. "If we find a spot off the road in the woods with a stream and a little bit of grass, that shall be enough for the horses. And we can take turns standing watch and sleeping in the coach."

It seemed as good a plan as any, although James didn't relish the thought of trying to maneuver the coach far enough off-road to be out of sight of passersby. It was not a particularly large vehicle, but neither was it small, nor intended for such rough driving. As he glanced forward, trying to ascertain the most likely spot, a flash of light caught his eye some distance farther down the road.

"Look ahead there," he said, pointing. "Is that a fire, or perhaps a building?" He pulled the team to a halt, to which the horses readily acquiesced, their heads hanging low with weariness.

"What if it's a village?" Sally sounded worried. "Perhaps we should turn back and follow that path we passed a bit earlier."

"It looks more like a single window or perhaps even a campfire," James said, searching the surrounding forest for any other glimmer of light but not finding any. "It's hard to tell, though—the trees are so thick here." Indeed, he rarely had seen such deep forest. It was quite unlike the more open woodland punctuating the farmers' fields back home, and though he never would have admitted it aloud, he found it a bit spooky, as if they'd suddenly been transported from the modern, civilized world of the mid-nineteenth century to the wild, untamed wilderness of two hundred and fifty years earlier, when the first Englishmen had settled upon the shores of the New World.

By now, Seamus was peering at the light as well. "Let me

run ahead and see," he said, hopping down and hurrying off along the road before either of the others could say a word.

"Oh, dear," Sally murmured as Seamus disappeared into the lowering darkness. "I hope he'll be all right."

Her voice shook slightly. Sally had always seemed determined and strong and unafraid, but James realized that the long day of stress had to be wearing on her. Even though he was not exactly easy in his mind himself, James found himself wanting to comfort her.

"Er, he shall be fine," he said awkwardly. "Seamus knows how to handle himself."

She shot him a brief smile, then turned to stare off into the gloom again. They sat there for what seemed a very long time without speaking again, only the breathing of the horses and the occasional jingle of their harness or stomp of a hoof breaking into the swelling symphony of the night creatures of the forest. The longer they sat, the more James's imagination took hold of him like a horse with the bit in its teeth. What if that light was a campfire belonging to their pursuers? What if Seamus stumbled into their camp without realizing it until too late?

But finally one of the horses lifted its head and snorted,

and a second later Seamus's pale face appeared in the road ahead. He climbed back onto the coach and explained breathlessly that the light belonged to a tiny homestead deep in the woods, consisting of a modest cabin and ramshackle but sizable barn.

"I peeked in the window, and there's only an old fellow and his wife having supper by the fire," Seamus reported. "Nobody else seems to be about."

At that, James felt a flicker of hope. "Good," he said. "Then perhaps we shall be able to manage to procure ourselves a quiet place to rest after all."

Sally looked alarmed. "What do you have in mind, exactly?" she demanded. "I'll not have you hurt anyone on my account."

"No! That's not what I meant at all." James blinked at her, a bit alarmed that she had so readily concluded that he intended some sort of violence toward the homesteaders. What sort of person did she take him for? "I was thinking I might approach them while you two stay out of sight," he explained. "I can try to use some of your father's down payment to bribe them into allowing the three of us to sleep in the hayloft or somewhere."

"What of the coach?" Sally asked. "If Winston and his thugs happen by and see it . . ."

"The barn is more than large enough to conceal it, and the horses, too," Seamus said. "It was too dark to see much when I tried to look in, but I did see a couple of mules and some sheep outside in a paddock nearby, so I expect there is room in there."

James nodded. "I'd also better offer enough money to convince them to keep word of our presence from anyone who might happen past in search of us." He shrugged. "I suppose I shall not have an opportunity to return any portion of the reward to your father anytime soon." He glanced at Sally, feeling troubled by the realization. As interested as he was in making his fortune, he did not want to do it unlawfully or at another's expense.

Sally put a hand on his arm. "Do not feel guilty," she said. "You have more than earned that reward in my opinion. Besides, Father has plenty of money—he shall not miss it."

The words didn't make him feel much better. But the touch of her hand did somehow, erasing the sting of her earlier comment.

"All right then," he said, setting down the reins and preparing to swing down from the coach. "I shall return in a moment."

Within an hour, all was settled. The old homesteading couple was inside their cabin, thrilled at suddenly having enough cash to buy supplies all through the coming winter. The horses were unhitched and munching away at the pile of hay James had purchased from the couple during their negotiations about the barn, and the coach was parked inside the broad barn doors, completely hidden from the road.

"That's that, then. We might as well try to get some sleep." Seamus stretched and yawned, glancing toward the rickety ladder leading up into the hayloft. "We may not have the chance to sleep this well again for a while."

"True enough." James glanced at Sally, feeling a bit awkward. This would be the first time on their journey that they were all sharing lodgings together instead of separating by gender at one inn or another. "Er, why don't you go up first?" he suggested uncertainly. "Take a few minutes to settle yourself for the night, and then Seamus and I will come up."

"Thank you. I shall not be long." Sally took one of the candles the old couple had provided for them and clambered swiftly up the ladder.

James and Seamus wandered over to the horses, making sure they had all they needed. "Do you think we can do this?" James asked quietly as he scratched one of the horses fondly on the neck. "Is it crazy to think we can escape these pursuers and then go west with little more than the clothes on our backs?"

Seamus shrugged. "It's no crazier than a lot of ideas people have," he said. "If people didn't do crazy things once in a while, take chances, then where would we be?"

His voice was uncharacteristically subdued, and James wondered if he was thinking about his father. Before he could figure out how to respond, he heard a voice calling their names softly from overhead.

He glanced toward the loft entrance and gasped. Sally was standing there at the top of the ladder, illuminated only by a thin shaft of moonlight streaming in through the barn's high windows. She was dressed in a pale linen chemise that ended just above her ankles. Her honey-colored hair streamed freely over her shoulders.

"Sakes alive," Seamus blurted out, staring openly. "Sally—you're a girl!"

James couldn't be certain in the dim light, but he thought she might have blushed. "Of course I'm a girl," she said sharply. "What did you take me for, Seamus—an owl? Perhaps a shoat or a toadstool?"

With that, she gathered her skirt and turned around, disappearing back into the loft. By the time the other two had climbed up there, she was lying on a soft pile of straw beneath one of the blankets the homesteaders had loaned them. James tried not to stare at her as he went about settling himself on another straw pile nearby.

It was true. They had known almost from the beginning that Sally was a girl. Somehow, though, it was a different matter entirely to *see* her dressed like one. And James found his heart was beating a bit faster than usual. . . .

Eleven

James slept deeply, untroubled by dreams. By the time he awoke, bleary-eyed and a bit disoriented, Sally was dressed once again in her boy's costume with her nightdress tucked away in her carpetbag and her hair beneath her hat. Seamus was already up as well and was sitting on a pile of harness, staring down at James.

"It's about time," he commented when James sat up and rubbed his eyes. "We thought you would sleep the day away."

James yawned. "I suppose I was wearier than I realized," he said. "No wonder, after all the excitement yesterday."

"Yes, we were discussing that," Sally spoke up. "As we have no real plan of action at this point, we were thinking we might head to Nauvoo, as it was mentioned in your aunt's clue. We can figure out a plan to continue west once we get there and procure some supplies."

For a moment James did not respond, his mind jumping

unbidden to the memory of Sally standing in the loft. But he shook off such thoughts.

"I suppose it's as good a plan as any," he said, busying himself with brushing the straw out of his clothes. "But our first priority at the moment should be to stay away from your pursuers."

They departed as quickly as they could harness the horses, who fortunately seemed none the worse from their extra efforts the day before. Soon they were making their way north and west, keeping a lookout for any sign of Winston and his cohorts. James couldn't help being especially nervous when the time came to cross the main road, which stood between them and Nauvoo to the north. But they were early enough that traffic was fairly light, consisting mostly of farmers and merchants who showed little interest in their passing. They made it across the intersection without incident.

"That's a relief," James said once he judged them safely away on yet another narrow, bumpy side road.

"Indeed!" Seamus exclaimed. "My heart was beating so loudly that I'm surprised that that Winston fellow couldn't hear it from wherever he is."

Sally shot him a worried look. "I still feel terrible for involving you both in all this," she said. "I had no idea it would turn out this way when I approached you in Washington that day. It was just so nice to speak with someone with similar interests, and you both seemed so nice. . . ."

At least until I turned her in, James thought, though he didn't say it aloud. He had no desire to remind her that he was the main reason they were in this situation.

"Never mind," Seamus assured her. "We *want* to help you get away. It's an adventure, isn't it, James?"

"That it is." James smiled tentatively at Sally. "We don't mind at all." Oddly enough, he found he meant it, somewhere down the line. . . .

Sally sighed, interrupting James's revelation. "Even so," she murmured, "thank you. Most people wouldn't be so understanding. Especially as many women of my acquaintance would probably find Mr. Winston Pace a fine catch." She shuddered visibly.

"Is he really so bad?" Seamus asked. "I mean, it's obvious he's an insufferable dandy, but . . ."

"That's not all." Sally shook her head. "If it were only

that, I might be able to tolerate him." She paused, looking dubious, as if doubting the truth of her last words. Then she shrugged and went on. "But while he seems mild-mannered enough in public, in private he's quite a boor. While he was courting me, he seemed utterly determined to crush my interest in abolitionism and women's rights." She clenched her slim hands into fists. "He even talked Father into refusing to allow me to travel to New York for the Seneca Falls Convention after I had already received his permission to go! That was when I knew I had to leave."

"The Seneca Falls Convention?" James repeated. "Do you mean that big ladies' meeting this past summer?" He vaguely recalled hearing a couple of passengers discussing the event while he was driving them somewhere in one of the coaches back in late July.

"It was much more than merely a ladies' convention," Sally said fervently. "It was convened by Lucretia Mott and Elizabeth Cady Stanton, who were present at the World Anti-Slavery Convention in London several years back, though they were denied seats by the conservative members of the abolitionist movement. That insult only increased their determination that equality should truly be for all—

including women. That is why they called a convention of their own this past July. They wished for a forum where all interested parties could discuss the social, civil, and religious conditions and rights of women."

Sally continued on after that, talking with enthusiasm about the cause of women's rights. Seamus nodded along, occasionally interrupting with a question or comment. But James merely listened silently. He was a bit surprised to hear Sally talk this way. She was certainly a different sort of creature from his sister, Eleanor, who seemed perfectly content to follow all the usual conventions of womanhood.

Perhaps Sally is a bit more like Aunt Ellie, for whom Eleanor is named but with whom she seems to have nothing in common, he thought.

Thinking of his aunt reminded him once more of those clues. He shifted the reins to his left hand and pulled the next letter out of his pocket. "Why don't we have a look at this," he suggested as soon as there was a break in the conversation. "Perhaps it shall give us some hint as to whether we are correct in heading toward Nauvoo."

"Good idea," Seamus agreed as Sally took the letter. "Read it out, Sally."

She cleared her throat and did so. As usual, the clue took the form of a few lines of verse.

A familiar starting ground
Lies in the land of ancient mounds
Travel westward 'cross the land
from the city of Moses and Abraham.

"It sounds rather specific, doesn't it?" Seamus commented, when Sally was finished.

"Does it?" James said with a frown. "To me it seems as if it is telling us only to continue to the West. Again."

It was getting harder and harder to shake the nagging feeling that the clues were merely some sort of elaborate word puzzle meant for amusement rather than any sort of real clues. Was he falling into the old Gates family trap of believing in possibilities that would never come to pass? Were they all being foolish even to consider following the directions in the verses? Once again, he found his mind returning to the obvious fact that his father had never done so himself, despite the fact that the verses had begun arriving several years earlier. Perhaps that was because Adam knew there were no riches to be found at the end of this particular trail; perhaps there was some earlier letter indicating as much that had not been in the packet. . . .

"Never mind," Sally said. "We might as well at least try to decipher it. What else have we to do while we ride?"

James couldn't argue with that. And after all, what harm was there in passing the time with this puzzle? Even if the letters led to nothing in the end, at least there was still that gold awaiting them in the West. So, they set about discussing the clue line by line, as usual.

"I can take a guess at the 'ancient mounds' thing, at least," Seamus said. A shadow of sadness crossed his face as he spoke. "My father told me all about the strange, ancient mounds that he and the Gates twins saw outside St. Louis during their travels. Perhaps we were meant to go to St. Louis after all?"

"Hold on," James said. "Ancient mounds? What do you mean?"

Seamus gave him a strange look. "Mounds," he repeated. "Built by some ancient tribe that lived in that area in the past. Did your father really tell you nothing of his adventures?" he asked in wonder.

James merely shrugged, his mouth hardening into a thin line. Did Seamus have to make so much of the rather obvious truth that Adam had shared almost nothing of his life with his youngest son? He wanted to blurt out as much, but held his tongue as guilt washed over him, making his skin feel hot. His own father might be far from perfect. But at least he was still alive, and James realized with some amazement that he was glad of that. But would he ever see him again?

Twelve

The trio discussed the clue on and off over the next several hours, though eventually all of them seemed to weary of it, as they could not decipher the meaning of the final line. They had found a good, fairly smooth road leading north-northwest toward Nauvoo, though it was a bit too heavily traveled for James's taste. He found himself glancing back nearly continually, well aware that dozens of people might be able to identify their coach if asked. It would have been helpful if there was some way to disguise the coach, and change the taller bay's crooked blaze to make it less distinctive. But neither Seamus nor Sally seemed worried overmuch about any of that, so James tried to keep his anxious cogitations to himself.

By the next morning, he had finally started to relax a little. But it was a moment too soon. They had hardly taken to the road when there came the sound of hoofbeats coming up behind them. James spun around, nearly dropping the reins as he spied a trio of horses—one chestnut, one bay, and one gray.

"They've found us!" he blurted out in a panic, ready to send the team forward.

Seamus turned to look, too. "You cutting a shine with us, my friend?" he said with a laugh. "I see nothing to worry over in the traffic behind us."

When he looked again, James realized that Seamus was right. There were two more horses trotting along behind the three he'd seen, and none of the riders were familiar in the least. All five were young men, at most four or five years older than James himself.

"Sorry," he said. "I thought—well, never mind."

By now the riders were upon them. One of them, a tall, gangly youth with jug-handle ears, pulled his mount to a walk beside the coach.

"Greetings," he called. "Do you know if this is the road to Hannibal, Missouri?"

"I regret to say I do not," James answered. "We are strangers to these parts ourselves."

The rider tipped his hat. "Well, never mind," he said. "I reckon we'll find it sooner or later. Are you by chance heading west to seek your fortunes in the gold mines?"

"Yes," Seamus answered, leaning over to address the rider. "Is that where you are going as well?"

A second young man had ridden up beside the first. "We are even now making our way to the Oregon Trail," he said eagerly. "We have heard that we can buy supplies in this Hannibal far more economically than we ever could have in St. Louis."

At that moment a sixth young man galloped up on a stout cob to join the group. "I've got it!" he called out. "I stopped back there to ask a farmer. He tells me we can be at the ferry to Hannibal by midday."

"Huzzah!" one of the others cried. "We're off then!"

"Do you mind if we follow you?" Seamus asked. "From what you say, this Hannibal sounds like the place to go for us as well."

James shot him a surprised glance. But the young men nodded agreeably. "We shall try not to ride too fast so your team might keep up," one of them said. "Off we go!"

"So we are going to this Hannibal?" James asked Seamus as the young men rode ahead, laughing and shouting to one another in high spirits.

Seamus shrugged. "We shall need supplies, shall we not? And Hannibal sounds as good a place as any to find some."

"True enough," Sally agreed. "Nauvoo might be as expensive as St. Louis. If Hannibal is smaller, it seems a better bet."

James wondered if the price of supplies was her only concern about going to Nauvoo. Perhaps she was anxious at the thought that a larger town might mean more likelihood of encountering Winston and his cohorts, who were surely still seeking them. For that reason, he gave in to the sudden change of plans without further comment.

However, his mind continued to race. Supplies were all very well and good, but the days were already growing noticeably shorter, and it seemed quite unlikely they would be able to travel very far into the Wild West before winter set in. If they wound up spending the winter in Missouri, how were they to support themselves? True, James still had a fair portion of Sally's father's money tucked away in his bag in the back of the coach. But what would they do if that ran out?

Such thoughts chased each other about through his mind like a dog after a hare. Among them he also found himself thinking more about his father and brothers. What would they think when he did not return as planned? Soon it would be clear they were not returning. Would they worry over him or only over the coach? He felt certain that Arthur, at least, would spare no thought for James but only complain at the loss of an expensive coach and two of their best horses. But would Adam feel regret for not paying more attention to James when he was around? What of Thomas, who had once been so friendly toward his youngest brother?

With distance, James found himself recalling those days more and more lately. Had his obsession over Charlotte turned Thomas irrevocably into a completely different person, or was that caring, fun-loving fellow still buried within him somewhere? James did not know, and, as the confusing thoughts and feelings tumbled through him, he tried to convince himself that he did not care.

As the young men had promised, they came within view of the Mississippi River just after noontime. James forgot about all else for a moment when he first set eyes upon the mighty river, which had to be a mile wide and sparkled in the midday sunlight like an expanse of glittering jewels. He had seen rivers before, of course, but none so immense that it seemed to cut the land in half. On the far shore, he saw a town—Hannibal, he presumed. Several impressive-looking steamboats were chugging along within view up or downriver, their smokestacks belching black puffs into the clear autumn air. A number of smaller crafts also plied the waters, seeming to zip about like insects beside the more deliberate procession of the grand paddle wheelers. For the moment at least, James's worries all fled his mind. Whatever else had happened or might yet, he was glad he'd come this far to see a sight such as this.

The ferry was about to depart and was nearly full. "You fellows go on," Sally urged the riders. "We shall catch the next one."

"All right, then." The lead rider tipped his hat to them. "We'll see you lads in the gold fields!"

The other young men let out a ragged cheer, and Seamus joined in with a laugh. James shaded his eyes against the sun and watched as the ferry made its way across the river.

Within the hour, another ferry had arrived to carry the coach across as well. James stood at the bow watching the far shore grow nearer. Many people said the Mississippi was the gateway to the West, and now as he crossed it, James couldn't quite shake the feeling that he was leaving everything he'd ever known behind and entering another world entirely—a vast new frontier filled with unknown dangers, but also unimagined wonders. He shivered, though whether with fear or anticipation, or merely due to the crisp river breeze, he could not have said.

"Say farewell to the States and regular civilization," Seamus said into James's ear, as if reading his thoughts. "And hello to the untamed West!"

By the time they disembarked from the ferry, James and his friends could see no sign of their earlier companions, so they decided to drive around a bit and get the lay of the land. Hannibal turned out to be a nice little port town, with most of the action happening on the riverside Water Street and a rather sleepy air enveloping the remainder of the village.

"We might as well go ahead and locate the general store," Sally said. "And then perhaps we can procure rooms at a boardinghouse. I believe we just passed one."

"In a moment." James had spotted a printer's shop just

ahead. There he was certain he would be able to purchase paper and a writing instrument to compose his letter home. "I just want to stop in here a moment."

"The print shop?" Seamus said as James brought the team to a halt in front of the building. "Why?"

"I want to write my father," James said as he swung down and tied the horses. "It is not fair to up and vanish without letting him know we have not been killed by wolves or some such. In addition, I wish to assure him that I shall pay him back for the coach and horses as soon as I make my fortune in the West."

"You will not tell him exactly where we are, or plan to go?" Sally asked with concern.

James shook his head. "Do not worry," he said. "I shall say nothing that might make it easier for your father to find us. Now come, let's finish this errand and then find lodging and something to eat."

They entered the shop, which smelled of ink and whale-oil lamps. The only person present was a young printer's apprentice, a slender boy about twelve years of age with a shock of unruly auburn curls and matching bushy eyebrows above sharp blue eyes.

"Can I help you?" the boy asked.

James explained his errand. "Do you have what I need?" he inquired when he was done.

"Of course," the boy replied. "I—"

"It's them!" a muffled shout rang out from just outside, interrupting him. "Those lads were right—they're here indeed, this is their coach. They must be in that shop right now!"

Seamus rushed over to peer out through the shop's front window. He gasped. "It's Winston!" he cried. "And he's got even more men with him this time!"

James spun around to look, hardly believing their bad luck. But was it truly luck? After all, he'd thought many times over the past day or two that they were not being nearly careful enough. Too late, wiser ideas tumbled through his head. Why hadn't they taken less populated roads, or traded the coach somewhere and continued by horseback, or traveled only at night?

But that didn't matter now. He stood rooted in horror, realizing that there was no escape this time. They were trapped! One of the men was at the horses' heads already— there was no way they could escape by coach this time. And on foot, in an unfamiliar town, with half a dozen determined men after them, there seemed little chance of any kind of getaway.

"Those gold-seekers must have told them we were here," Sally cried out in dismay.

By now Winston had spotted them through the windows. "Stay here, fellows," he called to his associates. "This shall not take long, I'll wager."

With a grin, he swaggered confidently toward the shop door, not even bothering to hurry. Seamus clenched his fists.

"We have to do something!" he cried. "Make a run for it!"

"What point is there in that?" Sally asked, for the first time sounding entirely weary and hopeless. "Can't you see that Winston's goons are armed? They look to be outlaws of the sort likely to shoot first and ask questions later. I won't have you risk your lives again for me." She took a step forward, sweeping her hat off her head to release her long hair. "I shall do my best to distract Winston long enough for you to get away. I'm sorry about the coach, but perhaps they'll leave it alone and you can return for it once we've gone." She shot them one last look, her blue eyes brimming with unshed tears. "Farewell, friends. And thank you for trying."

Without waiting for a response she turned away again. Then, squaring her shoulders and tilting her chin upward, she stepped toward the door.

Thirteen

"Sally, no!" James blurted out. Winston was almost at the door by now. He had just spotted Sally stepping forward, and his slimy grin had spread even wider across his narrow face.

Up until now, the young printer's apprentice had been observing all this with some confusion. But now he sprang into action.

"Come on," he hissed, grabbing James by the arm. "This way. If we hurry, I can get you all to safety!"

James hesitated for only the briefest moment. Strangely, the first thing that popped into his mind was that moment back in Baltimore when Sally and Seamus had gone along with his impulsive escape from Mr. Chandler without stopping to ask questions.

That was all it took to convince him. Taking Sally by the hand, he yanked her back away from the door. "Follow the boy," he said urgently.

The printer's apprentice was already dashing toward the

back of the shop with Seamus right behind him. James followed, still dragging Sally.

"Wait!" she cried. "We can't—"

"We can," James insisted firmly. "At least, we have to try."

She did not protest further, and he pushed her ahead of him through the back door.

Out front, the men were already shouting as they realized what was happening. Winston's voice was loudest among them as he ordered one of the men to stay with the coach so their quarry couldn't double back and escape that way, and for the rest to come with him. Just ahead, the printer's boy was ducking through a hole in a tall gate across the alley. Seamus paused just long enough to glance back and see that James and Sally were following, then ducked through himself.

The opening was narrow. The slender Sally had little trouble wriggling through after the others, but James had to jam his shoulders into the opening. Hearing the sudden cries of triumph as Winston and his cohorts spotted him gave him the extra impetus to burst through.

"Over here!" the printer's boy hissed just before he disappeared down another narrow alleyway.

James's heart pounded as he followed. The shouts behind them were far too close; he expected at any moment to feel a hand grasping him roughly by the hair or collar.

But the printer's apprentice was swift and clever, and it was obvious that he knew every back alley and side street in Hannibal. Before long, the shouts were growing fainter, angrier, and more confused. A few minutes later, they were barely audible at all.

The apprentice skidded to a stop before a tall, half-painted wooden fence. "We'll go through here," he said breathlessly. "It's all wild beyond. They'll never be able to track us in the woods."

"Let's go," Seamus agreed.

The boy grabbed a slat, which turned out to be loose. Pulling it to one side to create an opening, he waved the others through. Once on the other side, they found themselves in a small cleared area at the edge of a thick tangle of deep forest.

The boy ducked through the fence behind them, leaning back through just long enough to sweep their footprints away in the dry dirt on the other side and then letting the slat fall back into place. James nodded, impressed. Even if their pursuers tracked them this far, they would have no way of knowing where they'd gone.

Even so, they didn't slow down until they'd put at least half a mile of forest between themselves and the fence. Their guide moved just as swiftly and surely along a succession of animal trails and half-hidden dirt paths as he had in town. Before long they had taken so many twists and turns that James was quite certain that he himself couldn't find his way back to their starting point if his life had depended upon it.

Finally they stopped in a small, sun-dappled clearing surrounded by tall trees showing the last vestiges of their autumn glory. "All right," the printer's boy said. "I think it's safe to rest a bit if you like."

Sally stepped forward and grasped the boy's hands in her own. "Thank you," she said breathlessly. "Thank you so much. I cannot tell you how much this means to us, and I dearly hope that helping us shall not cause you any trouble."

"Well, I'll admit I still don't quite know what's going on. And I imagine my employer shall be mighty annoyed if he discovered I've left the shop untended this long." The boy tilted his head to one side and smiled. "But those fellers coming for you looked like no good, and I've always said that instinct is worth forty times knowledge." He winked. "By the way, I'm Samuel. Samuel Langhorne Clemens of Hannibal, Missouri."

Seamus collapsed onto a seat on a broad, flat rock. "Pleased to make your acquaintance, Samuel," he said, panting for breath. "I'm Seamus Poole of New York." He paused. "Well, formerly of New York, anyhow. I s'pose I'm not rightly from anywhere in particular these days."

James stepped forward to introduce himself before Seamus could think on that overmuch and turn gloomy. "And this is Miss Sally Chandler," he added. "That man back there means to marry her whether she likes it or not, with her father's blessing. Seamus and I have been helping her get away from the both of them."

"I see." Samuel rubbed his chin. "So you three city folk are on the run out here on the frontier, are you?"

Seamus frowned slightly. "Do not worry," he said. "James and I are not so helpless as it might seem. Our fathers were great explorers in their youth. In fact, they once traveled via some sort of raft all the way up the Missouri River just behind the famous Lewis and Clark, surviving only by their wits and having all manner of adventures along the way."

"Indeed?" Young Samuel looked intrigued. "Oh, do tell me more about it! I love nothing more than a ripping tale of the river. I hope to become a steamboatman myself one day."

"Very well." Seamus seemed mollified by Samuel's obvious interest. "It all began when James's Aunt Ellie decided she wished to join Captain Lewis's great expedition to map the wilderness. . . ."

After a while, with Seamus still talking, they climbed to their feet and continued on deeper into the forest. Once Seamus had exhausted his store of secondhand adventure tales, talk turned once more to their current journey. James explained to Samuel the details of their escape from Baltimore and subsequent experiences.

"So now," he went on, "we are thinking we might as well continue west and see if we might make a new life for ourselves there."

Seamus nodded eagerly. "We intend to make our fortunes in the newly discovered gold mines of California."

"Gold, eh?" Samuel said. "Sounds right exciting."

"Yes. But that's not the only wealth we hope to find out West. . . ." After only brief hesitation, James explained all about his aunt's letters. He could not have said exactly why he did, except that there was something eminently trust-worthy and intelligent about their new friend. And after the way he had saved them when all seemed lost, it seemed the least they could do was be completely honest with him.

When James mentioned they were stumped on the latest clue in the sequence, Samuel asked if he might have a look at the letter himself. When James handed it over, the boy scanned it and immediately nodded.

"Ah, yes," he said. "You have come to the right place to decipher this one, true enough."

"What do you mean?" Seamus asked eagerly. "Does it make some sense to you?"

"Perfect sense," Samuel replied. "For you see, this clue is indicating that you should come right here to Hannibal!"

Sally blinked. "It does?"

Samuel pointed to the last line of verse. "This bit—'the city of Moses and Abraham'—gives it away. You see, a Mr. Abraham Bird was the original owner of the site on which the town now stands. He received the land as recompense from the government for his losses in the New Madrid earthquake of 1812."

"I see," James said. "And Moses?"

"That is surely a reference to Moses Bates, who founded the town of Hannibal back in 1819. Oh, and we do have mounds in the vicinity as well—you have heard of the mound-building people who formerly inhabited this region?"

"Yes, a little." James was impressed by the boy's quick mind. "You certainly know a lot about the history of Hannibal, right down to the details of dates and such," he added. "Here we have been driving ourselves crazy over that line for days, and you cracked it right off."

"Indeed," Sally agreed with a smile. "However did one so clever as yourself wind up a mere shop assistant, Samuel?"

"I left school after my father died last year," Samuel replied matter-of-factly. "I am hoping to gain enough experience at the print shop so that I shall soon be able to help my older brother Orion at the newspaper he runs here in town."

Seamus looked a bit stricken by the news of Samuel's father's death, which surely reminded him afresh of his own loss. But James found himself more impressed than ever by their new friend. All his life, he'd felt sorry for himself for being so little understood within his family and having to work so hard for what little he'd ever had. But the more he saw of the wider world, the more fortunate he felt in having lived as comfortably as he had for so long, even if he hadn't realized it until now.

But he didn't ponder such things for long. Now that the initial excitement of the chase had passed, he realized that their situation looked more bleak than ever. They had no horses, no coach, no supplies, and only the little money in their pockets. Sally's pursuers were hot on their trail and would not give up easily now that they'd come so close once again. They couldn't stay in the woods forever, especially with the nights growing colder and their warmer clothing back in the coach, and Hannibal certainly wasn't large enough to hide them for long, no matter how well their new friend knew the place.

"We need to formulate a plan," James said. "What if we sneak aboard one of those steamships on the river and in that way put some distance between ourselves and Winston?"

Sally shook her head. "That won't work," she said. "Winston may be a scalawag, but he's not stupid. He'll already have a man guarding the docks."

James's heart sank as he realized she was right. Their pursuers knew they had no coach at their service any longer; they would be keeping a close watch on all public forms of transportation.

"What shall we do then?" he asked heavily. "Unless we go native and take to the woods permanently, it seems they have us one way or another. Especially as it is highly unlikely we can find passage to California until spring."

Samuel smiled. "Do not lose heart," he said. "I have an idea of where to seek help. . . ."

Fourteen

"I cannot believe spring is here at last!" Sally paused and took a deep breath of the warm air, which smelled of new grass, recent rainfall, and freshly turned soil. "Somehow, winter never seemed quite so long nor so cold back in Baltimore."

"That's the frontier for you, Miss." A tall, pleasant-faced, sandy-haired man finished tying a pack onto a sleepy, rawboned mule, then turned and smiled broadly at her, causing deep crinkles to form around his blue eyes. "I'm sure you have found that much in life is more difficult here than back East. And it shall only get worse as we head farther west. Sure you three don't want to rethink this adventure?"

"Absolutely not!" Seamus cried, so passionately that it made the man laugh.

James chuckled along. It was now early spring of the year 1849. He, Sally, and Seamus had spent the winter months living and working on the rural Clay County, Missouri, hemp farm of the Reverend Robert James.

That had been young Samuel Clemens's plan—or at least the result of his idea. On that day back in the autumn, he had left the trio hiding out in the woods long enough to return to town and seek out his older brother Orion's advice. As a newspaperman, Orion Clemens knew just about everyone in the area, and had quickly suggested that James and his friends contact his acquaintance Reverend James, who was in need of some help around the farm now that his wife, Zeralda, was busy with another pregnancy on top of caring for their infant son, Jesse, and five-year-old Frank. As Reverend James was a minister and well known in the community as an honorable man, the Clemens brothers thought he could be trusted to keep the runaways' secret. Besides that, the farm was comfortably far from Hannibal, and it seemed unlikely that their pursuers would be able to track them there unless someone purposely gave them away.

Once James and his friends had arrived, they had discovered that this plan was even more serendipitous than Samuel and Orion had realized, for Mr. James had just been invited to serve as chaplain on a wagon train heading west in the spring. He had been able to secure them places on one of the wagons, paying for passage with the little cash James had in his pockets and a gold-and-ruby ring that Sally had been wearing on a chain around her neck under her boy's clothes. With that settled, all they'd had to do was pass the winter without being discovered by their pursuers. Sally had even revealed her real identity, making life at least a little less complicated.

Even so, James had remained on alert at all times, looking over his shoulder at the slightest unusual sound; he could tell that Sally was equally jumpy. Things had improved slightly when, about a month after arriving on the farm, they'd heard from one of the family's slaves that Winston was rumored to have returned to the East. Even then they had not let down their guard, however. Several of the outlaw types they had seen with Winston that day were still skulking around Hannibal according to all reports, and Sally was convinced that they remained there on her father's orders.

"My father does not give up," she reminded James and Seamus. "He will never give up until I am back at home, or one or the other of us is in the grave."

But despite her gloomy prediction, the winter had passed without incident, and now the three friends found themselves preparing to travel to nearby Independence, Missouri, to meet up with a group of forty-niners heading west on the Oregon Trail. In addition to the pack mule, one of the James family's slaves had just led out another pair of mules pulling a farm wagon, which was already half-loaded with supplies for the trip. The slave, whose name was Jonah, would accompany them to Independence and help transfer the supplies into the covered wagons that would be taking them west, then return home with the empty farm wagon.

"I can hardly believe we are finally setting out," Seamus said, stepping forward to help Jonah hoist several fifty-pound packages of bacon into the wagon. "It seemed forever in coming!"

Reverend James picked up a bag of flour and stood there holding it, his gaze distant. "I still do not know if I am doing the right thing," he said. "I have prayed on it, but no answer seems forthcoming. And every time I look at my sons and think of leaving them for so long . . ." He sighed heavily and glanced toward the farmhouse, where young Jesse was playing with some wooden blocks on the porch.

Sally stepped forward and put a hand on the older man's arm. "Do not fret," she said gently. "Your wife knows that you are only making this journey for the good of your family. And your sons will recognize the same once they are old enough to understand. At this age, they will hardly notice you are gone before you are back again in a year or two."

"Thank you." The minister smiled at her. "That is what I keep telling myself. But it helps to hear it stated by someone else."

James smiled at Sally, marveling at how she always knew just the right thing to say. That was just one of the things he'd learned about her over the long, dark, cold winter. She glanced over and caught him staring. He quickly turned away and busied himself loading sugar, vinegar, beans, and lard into the wagon, a faint blush on his cheek.

As he helped the other men fill the wagon, he felt no small measure of pride in the weight of the supplies in his arms. Several months of hard work on the farm had earned the three of them not only their room and board but also enough extra cash to purchase supplies for the long journey. Even cautious James felt confident that they would have enough to get them there. Once they were in California it would be a different story, of course . . . but he was trying to take his cue from Seamus and Sally and not worry overmuch about that.

Sally had been busying herself sorting the smaller supplies, but once she finished with that task, she picked up a large tin of coffee and carried it toward the wagon. Seamus immediately hurried forward. "Here, let me help you with that," he insisted, taking it from her.

James frowned slightly, not particularly pleased by Seamus's gallantry. Over the past several months, the three of them had, by necessity, become much closer. James had found himself admiring not only Sally's way with words, but also her wit, kindness, and intelligence, not to mention the pleasing lines of her face and a certain ineffable quality to her blue eyes. He frequently caught himself staring at her, merely admiring the play of firelight on her pale hair—and on more than one occasion he had caught Seamus doing much the same thing. However, Sally treated both of them the same, and showed no signs of acknowledging any particular feelings from either direction. And for now, James was content with that.

"Come on." He slung a packet of woolen blankets into

the wagon and gave one last glance at the farmhouse, where Mrs. James and the two young boys were saying their good-byes to Reverend James. "I think we are just about ready to depart. And the sooner we're out of Missouri, the more comfortable I'll feel."

Fifteen

Indeed, James didn't relax until the wagon train had been on the trail for nearly a week. But with no sign of pursuit after that much time, his mind finally began to turn to other matters. All winter he had been too busy to think much of Aunt Ellie's clues, though he'd found himself pondering them or discussing them with his friends on the occasional evening in front of the fire.

Now, spending hours on end each day walking steadily beside the long line of lumbering wagons, he had plenty of time to think. By this time he and his friends had all committed the next clue to memory.

> Through a Courthouse too remote
> for any trial by jury;
> Round the nation's tallest Chimney
> (past Ash as refreshing as brandy).

"What do you suppose it means?" Seamus mused aloud as they tromped along one day through a dusty, hilly, open area with a broad, lazy stretch of the Platte River just to the north. "A courthouse—there's no such thing out here, is there? I mean, I know that the borderlands have their own sort of law, and I suppose the natives must have theirs as well. But a courthouse? I should not expect to see such a thing west of the Mississippi."

"Perhaps she means us to seek a courthouse once we reach California," Sally suggested. "Surely the Mexicans who settled the western coast practice some sort of justice."

"But would that be 'too remote for any trial by jury'?" James wiped his brow. The sun was growing warmer with each passing day, and this particular afternoon gave a hint of the full summer days yet to come. "True, it seems remote to us now. But while California may be sparsely populated, surely there are enough settlers there to drum up a jury if needed. Besides that, there are several more verses yet to come, so this one seems unlikely to provide the end point of the quest in any case."

Seamus shot him an amused look. "Logical as always, my friend," he said. "I do believe that is one reason Arthur found you so vexing, you know. You were forever countering his orders with logic."

James shrugged, waving his hand to shoo a pesky flying insect buzzing about his head. At the moment, Arthur—and everything else about James's old life back in Baltimore—seemed very far away.

As the days and weeks continued to pass, the wagon train made fine progress, with little trouble from the weather and even less from natives or wild beasts. Life on the trail fell into a steady rhythm. Early each morning, the wagon master would awaken everyone. After folding up their tents, James and his friends would set about assisting the other travelers in stoking the fire and making breakfast. Then it was time to gather up the grazing livestock, count the children to be sure none had wandered off, and hitch the mules and oxen. They traveled all day with only a short stop for lunch and rest; then, when dusk neared, the wagon master and the scouts would begin determining the best place to camp for the night. After circling the wagons for safety, everyone would build a fire in the center, and the women would cook dinner while the men saw to the livestock and set up their tents. After eating, the entire group generally lingered around the fire for a while, singing songs and trading stories until it was time to sleep.

It was a different way of life from anything James had ever known, but he found its discomforts were offset by its unforeseen benefits.

James had always been a person of many anxieties. He realized now that he had spent far too much of his time fretting over things he could not change or trying to plan things he could not control. So many of his waking thoughts had revolved around money—how little he had, how he could get more of it, what he would do with it if he did. But now, being out in the open air with a full view of the horizon on every side of him, he found himself gaining a different perspective on his life. In addition, walking all day and working hard, surrounded only by companions who shared the same goals, seemed to settle his mind somehow, perhaps by using up much of the energy he'd formerly put into other things. Before long he found that he often went hours—even days—without feeling uneasy about the loss of the coach, or what his father had thought when he'd received the letter he'd finally sent over the winter, or whether they would be able to find any gold in California. And when he did put his mind to something, such as Aunt Ellie's clues, it was easier to focus on it because his mind wasn't skittering off in a dozen different directions as it had previously.

One day as he walked a bit wide of the rest of the caravan, trying for a clearer view of the rugged landscape on all sides, James was the first in his little group to spot a solitary broad tower of rock on the horizon ahead. It rose from the flat earth, solid and immense, like some formerly magnificent but long ruined castle.

"Look up there!" he blurted out. "It looks like some kind of—I don't know—an ancient pyramid or something!"

Sally shaded her eyes with her hand. "It does," she agreed. "How odd! Then again, the landscape in this part of the continent is exceedingly odd. I never thought to find myself longing so for even a glimpse of a tree!"

Reverend James had been walking nearby, humming a hymn under his breath. Hearing them talking, he came forward to join them.

"What are you looking at?" he inquired.

Seamus pointed out the rock formation. "I wonder if it

is truly a natural outcropping, or perchance something more?" he said excitedly. "It does look a great deal like a pyramid, and everyone knows that is a favorite symbol of the Freemasons who have controlled so much of this nation from its inception. And it is most odd to see such a thing standing there all alone. What if it is actually something the government back in the States has chosen to conceal from people? Some secret outpost, or the remains of a more advanced civilization . . ."

Several others walking nearby, alerted by the loud voices, wandered over out of curiosity. One of them, a grizzled old man known only as Hank, laughed upon hearing Seamus's speculation.

"'Fraid not, sonny," he said. "I was chattin' with Beau yesterday—he's scouted on two or three of these treks already, as ye may know—and he reckoned we'd be coming up on this sometime today. Says it's known as Courthouse Bluff. That other one near it's called the Jailhouse." He pointed with one stubby, tobacco-stained finger at a second bluff that had just become visible as they walked on.

"Oh." Seamus frowned slightly, as if disappointed. Then he shrugged. "Well, I suppose that's all right, then.

I wonder why they call it . . ." His voice trailed off, and he gasped.

James shot him a stern look. He had connected the outcropping with Aunt Ellie's letter as soon as the other man had mentioned the name. But he didn't want to speak of it aloud until he and his friends were alone.

"What is it, son?" Reverend James asked Seamus with concern. "You look most odd all of a sudden."

"N-no, nothing," Seamus stammered, shooting James a furtive glance in return. "Er, I just swallowed a gnat, that's all."

Once the others had wandered off, the three friends discussed what this might mean. "Surely this Courthouse Rock is what Ellie references in her verse," Sally exclaimed. "That means we are on the right trail!"

"True, though what other trail could there be if we are indeed meant to go west?" James shrugged. "It's beginning to seem that Aunt Ellie is merely describing her own journey west rather than providing us with any sort of enlightenment as to our quest."

"Not entirely," Seamus pointed out. "As Sally says, at least this shows that we are going the right way. And that, my friend, is progress."

James still wasn't completely convinced that the letters were anything more than an idle puzzle. But he had to admit that Seamus had a point.

Some days later, James looked up at the sound of hoof-beats and saw one of the scouts riding back toward their wagon, which happened to be near the end of the train on this particular day. "We're stopping just over the next hill for the night," the scout reported. "Cap'n Stallard thinks it looks like rain and wants to set up camp early."

"All right. Thanks." James glanced over at Reverend James, who was walking beside him. "Ready for a rest, sir?"

"Aye." Reverend James stretched both arms over his head. "Rain or no rain, I'll sleep well tonight."

As the wagon crested the hill, James saw that the earlier wagons were already maneuvering into a large circle. Several of the children were already running about, under the watchful eye of the older women, seeking firewood.

"Looks like they're rushing to beat the rain," Sally commented, hurrying up beside James. "I'd better go help."

James paused just long enough to watch her gather her skirts and run down the hill, as fast and free as if she were still dressed in her boy's clothes. Then, hearing Seamus call for his help in leading the mules, he turned away and went to work.

Before long the scent of woodsmoke mingled with cooking beans and coffee. Though the gathering clouds dulled the colors of the sunset, the threatened rain was holding off for the moment. Soon the entire camp was gathered around the roaring fire.

James helped himself to a serving of beans and then joined Sally and Seamus, who were sitting a little apart from the others on some flat rocks. He settled himself beside them and ladled a spoonful of piping-hot beans into his mouth.

"We were just discussing the letters," Seamus told him. "I think it's time to pull out the next one. We've seen everything referenced in the previous one, I reckon."

James nodded, having been thinking much the same thing since leaving the idyllic spot known as Ash Hollow earlier that day, soon after fording the wide, but shallow, Platte River to reach the north side.

"Ash Hollow—that would have to be the 'Ash as refreshing as brandy' from the verse," Sally said, stirring her dinner. "There is no question that the freshwater we found there was most refreshing, particularly after the hot, dry weather of these past few days. The sight and shade of the trees was most refreshing, too. I don't think we've seen a proper tree in a hundred miles."

Seamus was nodding, though he seemed to have little interest in discussing the pleasures of Ash Hollow. "And we had the remote Courthouse days ago," he put in eagerly. "And the 'nation's tallest Chimney' soon after. That's the whole verse, right?"

Indeed, they had passed another incredible outcropping, this one known as Chimney Rock, some dozen miles west of the Courthouse and Jailhouse. If anything, it had been even more impressive to see its tall, narrow spire stretching hundreds of feet over the plains.

"All right," James agreed. "As soon as I'm finished eating, I shall—"

He was interrupted by a sudden flurry of angry shouts from nearby. "Over here!" a voice yelled shrilly. "Some scoundrel's trying to steal our food!"

Sixteen

James leaped into action along with most of the other men. He was one of the first to reach the man who had shouted the warning. Chet Hawkins was a tall, hot-tempered gold-seeker from Kentucky, a man always ready for a drink or an argument. He was now holding tightly to a small, wriggling figure.

"Let me go!" the would-be thief sobbed. "Please, sir— I didn't mean any harm!"

James stepped forward. By the flickering light of the fire, he saw that the thief couldn't be much more than ten years old. "It's just a boy," James said. "Easy, Chet. I don't think he'll do much harm."

"Not if I have anythin' to say about it," the man growled. "Where you sneak in here from, boy?"

The boy's eyes were wide with terror. "I didn't mean any harm," he repeated. "My family is camping down the river." He waved one small hand, vaguely indicating a westerly direction.

By now more of the group had reached them. "Bet I know where he's from," a man called out. "Must be one of them Mormons!"

"Always figgered they was trouble," another man muttered, several more in the group murmuring in agreement.

James, along with the others, had often caught sight of Mormon pioneers making their way west along their own trail on the north side of the river. "Is that true?" he asked the boy in a friendly tone. "Are you with the Mormons?"

The boy stared up at him for a moment, then nodded. "I didn't mean any harm, sir," he said once again. "We had to leave home quick, and we didn't pack enough sugar. I just came to see if you'd any to spare." His face crumpled. "I know it was wrong, but I didn't think you'd miss it. You have so much more than us. . . ."

"Sounds like a confession to me," Chet snapped. "Let's show this ragamuffin what we do with thieves!"

A ragged cheer went up from several of the men. But James placed himself in front of the boy and stared down the crowd with a scowl.

"Don't be idiots," James said sharply. "He's just a child.

What do you mean to do, string him up for daring to have a sweet tooth?"

By now Reverend James was pushing his way forward through the crowd. "What's all this, then?" he inquired in his mild way. When several of the bystanders filled him in, the minister immediately stepped forward to stand beside James. "Let's be reasonable, men," he said. "Isn't forgiveness a Christian virtue?"

"We ain't dealing with no Christian, pastor," a man called out, frowning at the boy.

Still, the tide of sentiment seemed to have turned with the arrival of Reverend James. There was some additional grumbling, but even Chet didn't seem to have much more to say. Within moments the boy was released. He scurried off, disappearing instantly into the darkness.

James was halfway back to the campfire when Sally rushed up to him. "James!" Sally cried, rushing up to him. "I can't believe I missed what just happened. But I heard you were positively glorious!"

"I was?" James blinked at her, pleased but confused by the enthusiasm of her reaction. "Er . . ."

She grabbed him and hugged him tightly.

James was a bit distracted by the feel and smell and idea of her so close to him. Her golden hair tickled his nose, and he felt oddly light-headed for a moment. But he managed to stammer out something about doing what he thought was right.

Sally let go of him and stepped back just seconds before Seamus appeared. It was soon evident that he, too, had just been apprised of what had happened.

"Figures I'd miss all the excitement," he said. "When I heard that shout, I thought it must be wolves or something." He grinned sheepishly. "Didn't think a city boy like me would be much good in a pinch like that, so I took my time responding."

"No, it was only a hungry, helpless Mormon child hoping for a bit of help from us." Sally was still smiling admiringly up at James. "Our friend here was his champion and convinced the others to show mercy and send him on his way."

"Well, Reverend James had a bit to do with it as well. . . ." James mumbled, beginning to feel rather bashful in the face of such effusive praise.

Sally hardly seemed to hear him. She clasped her hands together. "You were just like one of the brave abolitionists or Elizabeth Cady Stanton or someone like that—standing up for one with no voice!" she cried. "It's marvelous to see that you care so much about fairness and your fellow man, James. After all, as long as one group is ill-treated, all humanity suffers."

James hadn't really thought about any of that—he had merely taken pity on a small, frightened face and acted as he thought right. But he wasn't about to say so—not with Sally gazing at him with such admiring eyes!

"I would have hurried over sooner had I known the thief was a Mormon," Seamus said as they all returned to their dinners. "I would have liked to ask him if he knows anything of William Morgan's so-called widow."

James realized he'd hardly heard Seamus mention Mr. Morgan, the Freemasons, or any other talk of conspiracy in the past several days. Had the much more tangible adventure of their current pursuit finally begun to chase such silly notions out of his head?

"Don't be ridiculous, Seamus," Sally said, leaning over to toss a stray branch onto the fire. "The boy was little more than a toddler. I'm sure he would know nothing of such speculative matters."

James didn't bother to correct her impression of the boy's age. He still wasn't sure what to think of the whole incident, but he was certain of one thing: it was nice to have so much of Sally's attention.

It wasn't until the following day that conversation returned to Aunt Ellie's clues. As the three friends trudged along, doing their best to avoid the dust kicked up by animal hooves and wagon wheels, James pulled the next letter out of his pocket.

"Here, I'll read it out," Sally offered, taking it from him. She proceeded to do so:

'Round a bluff toward Independence
Lies a twisting, winding snake.
When you find yourself a raft,
that's the path that you should take.

Seamus looked alarmed. "Independence?" he said. "Hold on, is that referring to Independence, Missouri? But we left there at the *start* of this journey!"

"That is odd," Sally commented. "Although perhaps she

is only referring to a feeling of independence at escaping the restrictions of the States in continuing farther west?"

Seamus waved one thin hand in dismissal. "That can't be it," he scoffed. "These verses aren't about things like that. They're meant only to help us find whatever hidden wealth she's leading us toward."

"You know, I wonder if we should be assuming that that is entirely true," James spoke up, giving voice to the thoughts that had been troubling him almost from the beginning of this quest. "What if that's not the purpose of Aunt Ellie's notes?"

"What do you mean?" Sally asked.

"It's just that we do not really know what the messages are truly about," James said. "For all we know, it could be just a word game—one not really meant to lead anywhere. Just a puzzle for Father to solve in front of the fire on an evening."

"It can't be," Seamus answered immediately. "Not with the history of treasure hunting in your family, James. What true Gates would pull something like that?"

Resentment flooded through James at the very mention of the phrase "treasure hunting"—not to mention the implication, however unintended, that James was not a true Gates because he was not obsessed with treasure hunting for its own sake. But he bit his tongue, determined not to lose track of his point due to such useless emotion.

"Just think about it," he said instead. "What point would there be in this sort of complexity and obfuscation? Why would Aunt Ellie not simply uncover the, er, treasure herself?"

"Perhaps she wanted to share it with your father," Sally suggested.

James shrugged and kicked at a rock on the trail. "All right," he said. "But why then wouldn't she unearth it herself, divide it as she wished, and send it along with a trusted messenger? Or at least more directly insist that he come west to retrieve it? Why send a whole series of encoded letters that could be so easily lost or intercepted? It seems unnecessarily risky—not to mention time-consuming."

"Gold!" Seamus's face brightened so dramatically that for a moment James thought he'd spotted a vein of the precious metal right there along the dusty trail. "That must be it. Remember? We've always theorized that she might have found a vein or nugget out there in California. She is an old lady, and her husband was surely quite feeble even at the time she began writing those letters."

Sally nodded with interest. "I see," she said. "You are saying she might have discovered gold in California long before Mr. Marshall found it at Mr. Sutter's mill. But she wasn't able to extract it herself, so she sent these coded messages to her brother, Mr. Gates, asking for his help."

James had to admit it was an interesting theory. "I suppose you could be right," he said slowly, hope flickering within him once more. Perhaps his earlier dreams of wealth and success were not completely out of the question after all. "Anything is possible."

"Good." Seamus smiled. "Now let's get cracking on the clue. If Independence does not refer to the town in Missouri, what else do you think it might mean?"

Over the course of the next few weeks, they deciphered that portion of the verse and the rest as well. They passed the immense Independence Rock a few days after the Fourth of July and paused there to carve names and messages into its granite surface, just as many other travelers had done before them. Some days after, they had arrived at a trading post on the Snake River, where the wagon train split into two groups. A small number of travelers headed northwest along the Snake toward the Oregon Territory, while most of the company—including James and his friends—went to the southwest at a tributary known as the Raft River.

"I suppose that means we are still going the right way," Seamus had pointed out when they'd reached the Raft. "Ellie seems to say that this is the path we should take."

After that, several days of thunderstorms had followed, keeping them too busy to think more of the quest. By the time the weather had settled down again, they were at the foot of the Sierra Nevada Mountains, surely one of the most impressive sights James had seen in all his life. It was a long, arduous journey through the first section of the Sierras, but James found much to appreciate about the interesting landscape through which they were traveling.

He also found himself already looking back nostalgically upon his cross-country journey, even though it was not yet over. He felt he'd become a different person during the course of the long, difficult trek—a new James, brave and calm and sensible and strong; a James much superior to the old, fearful, fretful one. More importantly, he found himself wondering what Sally would wish to do once she reached the end of this trail. The two of them, along with Seamus, had been a team throughout this adventure. But would that continue? Or would they all go their separate ways? Being with Sally, trying to be the type of man she expected of him, was such a large part of his new self that James couldn't imagine what he might do or feel if that were the case. . . .

Despite such growth, however, James felt more and more of his usual anxiety creep back as they drew nearer to their destination—the gold miners' camp near Sutter's Mill known as Dry Diggins, or, more recently, Hangtown. In chatting with his fellow travelers along the way, he had learned that many forty-niners had opted against the long, difficult overland journey they were making, choosing instead to travel from the East Coast to California by ship around South America or, in some cases, to the Isthmus of Panama, where they then trekked across and sailed again on the opposite coast. It had not taken him long to realize that this could be Mr. Chandler's plan if he suspected his daughter might be heading for the West Coast. All he would need to do was send a few of his thugs, who could in turn hire whatever number of outlaws were needed to search for any news of Sally among the mining camps springing up near the gold deposits.

Before long the scouts estimated that they were only a day's journey outside of Hangtown. That was when James cautiously brought up the topic with his friends.

"I think we shall need to be careful when we arrive once more among other people," he said after explaining his concerns.

Sally nodded. "I have been thinking much the same," she admitted softly. "As I said, Father is not a man who loses gracefully. Even if Winston has given up on me by now, there is no doubt in my mind that Father will keep looking until he finds me, or spends his entire fortune trying."

James shot her a sympathetic look. At one time he might have thought it a blessing to have such a concerned father, particularly one who also happened to be so wealthy. After coming to know Sally and her nature, however, he could see that something that might seem a blessing to one could be a curse to another. Perhaps no family was perfect, but James was coming to realize that his own might not be so terrible as he'd always believed.

The next day, as predicted, they reached the outskirts of Hangtown. It was a rough, dusty, sprawling settlement consisting of numerous hastily erected tents and lean-tos along with more permanent buildings such as the inn and trading post. There was a huge old oak tree near the center of town with a rope noose dangling from one stout limb, leaving little doubt as to the origin of the camp's name. Among the place's other notable features were the random large holes found here and there where·forty-niners had decided to dig for gold in the street.

Most of the newly arrived travelers immediately set about finding lodging or seeking news on the latest gold discoveries. But James and his friends bid a quick farewell to Reverend James and their other companions and then hung back by the wagons, collecting their gear, which was much lighter now after months on the trail. Sally had donned her boy's clothes before arriving, away from prying eyes. So she earned no particular notice in the largely male-populated mining camp. After a quick stop at the trading post to replenish their supplies of food and drink, the three friends hiked out of town into the hilly woods on foot.

"Better if we keep out of sight for a while," James said, "until we figure out whether anyone might be looking for us."

Seamus nodded, though as he glanced over his shoulder toward the bustling settlement he looked slightly impatient, perhaps thinking of all the gold waiting to be found. "All right, then let's set up our own camp," he said. "While you two check for trouble from Sally's old man, I'll start scouting for spots to start digging or panning. I heard the best area to start is south of town at Cedar Ravine." He led the way down a narrow trail through the woods, walking fast despite all the gear he was carrying.

"I can hardly believe we're really here, in the midst of gold country." Sally smiled as they walked, her cheeks pink with excitement. "In one sense it seems like a lifetime ago we were leaving Baltimore, but at other moments it feels like only yesterday!"

James shifted his heavy pack to his other shoulder and nodded. "I know what you mean," he said, smiling back at her. "I wonder what everyone back home—"

Just then, Seamus let out a strangled yelp from a few

yards ahead. The folded tent he was carrying fell to the ground with a clatter.

"What's wrong?" James asked, leaving Sally and hurrying forward.

He stopped short when he reached Seamus's side and saw exactly what was wrong. They were now staring into the dripping jaws and beady brown eyes of a massive grizzly bear blocking the trail not five feet ahead!

Seventeen

James stood frozen in place, knowing that he should grab one of the weapons stowed in the pack still on his back. But somehow he was unable to do so.

So this is it, he thought numbly. *We escaped from Sally's father, we made it all the way across the continent, through rough terrain, difficult weather, hostile native territories, and the threat of illness. And now it's all going to end at the claws and teeth of this wild creature. I only hope Sally can manage to get away while it's distracted by mauling us. . . .*

"Ben!" a gruff voice shouted suddenly from somewhere behind the bear. "Leave 'em alone, you ol' galoot. They've no grub for you!"

James blinked, confusion breaking through his terror. The bear flicked its ear, then turned its enormous head to look behind itself. With a grunt, it backed up a few steps.

It was only then that James saw the man hurrying

toward them down the narrow forest trail. He appeared to be in his forties, with a weather-beaten face nearly hidden by a full beard and mustache. He was dressed in a buckskin jacket and pants and carried a long rifle.

"You all right, kids?" the man called out in a friendly manner.

"Uh, we're fine," James called back, a bit embarrassed to realize that his voice shook as he said it. Clearing his throat, he tried again. "Were you—how did you—"

If the man noted James's discomfiture, he gave no indication of it. As James watched in shock, the man casually pushed past the bear—which grunted again but didn't protest further—and stuck out one hand.

"My name's Adams, James Capen Adams, to be all preciselike," he said. "But most folk' round here know me as Grizzly."

James shook his hand, still a bit stunned by this turn of events. "Hello," he said. "I'm, uh . . ."

"He's James Gates. That's Sal—er, Sam Chandler back there, and I'm Seamus Poole." Seamus pushed past James, taking the man's hand and shaking it vigorously. "Thank you for saving us! But shouldn't we do something about, er, you know . . ." He gestured vaguely toward the bear.

Grizzly Adams tilted his head to one side. "Do something?" he replied, scratching his chin through his beard. "Like what, now?"

"Er, uh . . ." Seamus glanced from the bear to the man's rifle and back again, seeming confused.

Adams let out a hearty laugh and slapped a hand over his heart. "Oh, I'm just funnin' ya, boy! Fact is, this scoundrel here's my best friend and constant companion, Benjamin Franklin. Ben to his friends. Had 'im since he was a cub." Adams reached over and scratched the bear on the shoulder. Ben was now sitting on his haunches sniffing curiously at something on the ground.

"You have a pet bear?" Seamus sounded astonished, and James knew exactly how he felt. He'd seen smaller bears from a distance in the woods and fields back home, of course, and even some larger ones such as this one in the traveling menageries that sometimes toured the East Coast. But this wild creature showed no signs of wanting to run away like the bears in Maryland, and there were no metal bars separating it from them.

Despite its size and strength, however, the bear seemed harmless enough sitting there on the trail like some shaggy, oversize hound. As the trio chatted with Adams, James almost managed to forget the beast was there. Sally joined them, her eyes wide.

"I ain't seen you three around here before," Adams said. "You come in with the last wagon train?"

"We did," Sally replied, her voice taking on the deeper tone of "Sam." "Like everyone else, we are hoping to find gold in these hills."

James glanced over, surprised by the note of eagerness in her voice. Though she had always expressed some interest in the California gold, he had thought her much more focused on escaping and starting a new life far away from her father's clutches. Then again, perhaps arriving in Hangtown had ignited a stronger interest in her—it was certainly easy enough to get swept up in the general enthusiasm that permeated the place. He already found himself glancing down at every rock and pebble, hoping to spot a glint of gold in the sunlight.

"Ah! Tryin' yer hands at some prospectin', are ye?" Adams said. "Got yourself a likely stake yet?"

Seamus stepped toward him, apparently forgetting all about Ben in his excitement, as he nearly trod on the bear's paw. "No, we just got here," he said. "Can you tell us where we might have the most luck?"

Adams leaned on the butt of his rifle. "Aye," he said. "Think I might be able to advise ye there. . . ."

"It was lucky that we ran into Grizzly," Seamus commented as he crouched beside a stream the next day. He stuck his pan under the water and scooped up a portion of the river-bed, carefully sifting it just as the owner of the trading post had showed them when they'd bought their prospecting supplies.

James grimaced, remembering the close encounter with their new acquaintance's "tame" bear. "It might not have been so lucky had his friend Ben been a little farther ahead of him on the trail."

"Don't be silly, James," Sally chided, wading farther into the stream to dip her pan. "From what I understand, bears are really not the terrible, carnivorous beasts some believe them to be. They generally feed on nuts and berries and such."

"Oh? And how would you know of such things, living in the heart of Baltimore with nary a bear in sight?" Seamus teased.

Sally tossed her head, nearly loosening her boy's cap. "Have you never heard of books, my friend?" she teased in return. "Perhaps if you had, you might be a bit better at panning for gold. You're letting the water run out too fast!"

James chuckled at their banter, but inside he felt a flash of unease. He and Seamus had been through so much with Sally that it was easy to forget that she was from a much higher social class than they were, and that even as a girl she had received a much better education. Their lives had been far different before fate had brought them together on this cross-country odyssey.

But he put those thoughts aside, being more and more preoccupied lately with a different matter. "I only wish I knew where to find my Aunt Ellie," he said, swishing his pan without paying much attention. "All I know is that she lives somewhere in California." He sighed and glanced down at the few dull, ordinary rocks left behind once the water and smaller grit had washed away. "I even checked the most recent letter to make sure, and there's no real address indicated."

"Oh, I nearly forgot about the letters in all the excitement of arriving," Seamus commented. "It's the final one, correct? We ought to look at it and see if it can indeed tell us where to search for gold, in case this spot does not provide any."

James shrugged. "It's the last letter we *received*," he corrected. "We have no way of knowing whether there are more arriving in Baltimore even now. Come to think of it, that could be another reason why my father had done nothing with the verses yet—he was waiting until he had all the clues before setting out."

Seamus seemed little interested in such cautions. "So where is it?" he demanded impatiently. "Let's hear the next clue."

James fished the letter out of his pocket. Soon Sally was reading the clue out loud as usual.

Close your Mission if you dare
'neath Mr. Todd's most glorious Bear.
Near three hills 'tween sea and creek
find the Treasure whom you seek.

"Hmm," James said thoughtfully. "It seems rather specific, yet still no clearer than any other."

"'Close your mission,'" Seamus commented. "Do you suppose that means we are at the end of the quest?"

"It might." Sally shrugged and handed the letter back to James. "But then again, it might not. The word 'close' could mean any number of things."

They discussed the clue for the remainder of the day while they worked. By the time the sun set over the western hills, they had found neither gold nor answers. They trudged back to their little camp and found their new friend Grizzly Adams perched on a log there. Ben was stretched out on the ground nearby, snoring loudly. The sight of the big creature still gave James the chills.

"Started to think the wolves musta got ya," the mountain man said by way of greeting. Then he stood and stretched. "Find yourselves any gold today?"

"Not yet," Seamus admitted. "But we're making good progress. And so far we are the only ones in this part of the stream. Thanks to your advice, I'm sure we'll discover something tomorrow!"

Adams grinned and winked. "That's what I like," he

said. "A boy with some optimism! Anyway, I was thinking of toddling into town for a nip and some grub at the saloon. Care to join me?"

James hesitated, not sure that was a good idea. He already felt conspicuous enough now that they were back among settlements once again. Everywhere they went, he found himself looking for Mr. Chandler's goons out of the corner of his eye. How much more conspicuous would they be walking into Hangtown in the company of Adams, with Ben lumbering along at their heels?

But both Seamus and Sally did not seem worried. They were already agreeing eagerly to the plan. Apparently they were more concerned with a hot meal at the end of their long day than with anything else.

James was glad enough of that once he had a belly full of meat and drink. Ben had stayed outside, and the saloon was crowded and noisy enough that their little party of four seemed unlikely to draw notice. Adams was keeping them all entertained with rousing tales of his years in the wilderness hunting and trapping, and taming bears and other wild beasts to sell to menageries and others.

After a while Adams interrupted his own storytelling to

roar out a greeting to a tall bronze-skinned man near his own age who had just entered the establishment. "Pomp!" he exclaimed. "You old rascal. Where you been hidin' yerself? Didn't strike it rich and not tell your ol' friend Grizzly, did 'ja?"

The man came over and shook Adams's hand. "Greetings, my friend," he replied in a surprisingly cultured voice. "I see that pet bear of yours hasn't eaten you yet, hmm? Thought I spotted him lurking outside frightening the new miners." He smiled at James and the others. "Ah, and I see you're busy frightening some newcomers yourself. Welcome to Hangtown, young friends. I'm Jean-Baptiste Charbonneau, but you can call me Pomp."

James introduced himself and his friends. But Seamus hardly seemed to hear. He was staring at the newcomer with a very odd look on his face.

"Charbonneau!" he cried out, his eyes brightening. "Of course! I knew I recognized the name. Are you by chance related to the Charbonneau who was part of the expedition of Lewis and Clark?"

Pomp looked startled. "Why, yes," he said. "My father was hired by the Corps of Discovery as a translator and guide, and my mother came along. In fact, I was born during the journey."

"Indeed?" Seamus said. "Ah, then it seems your mother was the intelligent native girl, Sacagawea, who helped our fathers escape danger and return to Massachusetts!" He gestured to James and himself.

James was confused. But as Seamus chattered excitedly with their new acquaintance, he started to catch on.

It seemed that this man's parents had not only been part of Lewis and Clark's expedition, but that his mother had helped guide Adam and Ellie Gates and Franklin Poole back to the East at the end of their adventure. Once again, he found himself astonished by how much Seamus knew of those days compared to what little he knew himself.

"My, my. That's certainly a fine coincidence!" Adams said as the story came out, seeming immensely amused by the whole situation. "What are the odds, d'you suppose? You all meetin' up here like this, that is?"

"I'm not the gambler you are, Grizzly," Pomp joked. "You'll have to tell me."

He sat down to join them, and the conversation flowed

long into the evening. By somewhere around midnight, it seemed the most natural thing in the world for James and the others to share Aunt Ellie's latest letter with their new friends. And so it was, with their help, that they were finally able to decode its meaning.

"This bit must be referring to the Bear Flag Revolt of three years back," Pomp said, pointing to the second line.

"Of course!" Adams slapped the table so hard that their mugs jumped. "Mr. Todd—that must be that Todd fellow who designed the flag of the short-lived California Republic. Always thought he had right fine taste in symbols." He roared with laughter at his own joke.

Clearly seeing that the younger three were confused, Pomp quickly explained. "Our friend here approves because there was a bear as part of the design," he said. "It was created by a man of my acquaintance, William L. Todd, and flew over Sonoma Plaza for the monthlong existence of the Bear Flag Republic, which only ended when California officially became American territory."

"All right," James said. "But what does this tell us of our quest?"

Pomp shrugged. "Well, it refers to a 'Mission' as well as

the Bear Flag," he said. "I'd wager that to find this treasure of yours, all you need is to travel to *La Mision de San Francisco Solano de Sonoma*. That's the Spanish mission in Sonoma— just under one hundred miles from here."

Eighteen

Even after the late night at the saloon, James awoke early the next morning feeling restless. "I think we should go to Sonoma and finish the quest," he said as soon as the others awoke.

Seamus rubbed his eyes and yawned. "All right," he mumbled. "Soon as we find some gold, we can use part of it to hire some horses to take us to Sonoma."

"No. I mean I want to go now. Today."

Sally looked surprised. "Are you certain?" she asked. "You've said yourself on more than one occasion that you don't believe there's anything important at the end of the trail. *If* this is indeed the end."

"Right," Seamus agreed. "Why the sudden change of heart?"

James hesitated, not certain how to respond. "I just need to know for sure," he said at last. "We can take a quick trip to Sonoma, then return and get back to our prospecting. Besides," he added hastily as another argument in his favor occurred to him, "it will take us out of range for a while in case anyone is looking for us here in the gold fields."

Sally pursed her lips, looking thoughtful. But Seamus shook his head.

"It's just not a good idea," he said. "If we leave, we risk losing our stake. There are more Argonauts arriving nearly every day."

"That's true," Sally said softly. "We could go to Sonoma later, when winter comes."

"I don't want to wait that long. We are so close; why not put it to rest once and for all?"

Seamus narrowed his eyes. "Hang on a moment, James," he said. "Aren't you the one who's always saying you don't believe in all that treasure hunting nonsense? You always say your family members were foolish to waste so much time upon such things. Is this your Gates blood coming through at last?"

"It's not about that," James insisted, annoyed that Seamus was being so difficult. "I just don't like to give up when we're so near to an answer. And you heard Mr. Charbonneau last night—we could leave today and be back here inside the month."

"Doesn't matter." Seamus's expression remained stubborn. "You can go if you like, James. I'm not losing my chance at finding gold just because you've finally decided to take up the family obsession."

"I'm not . . ." James cut himself off and took several deep breaths, not wanting to let Seamus get to him. If he was going to be so irrational about this, perhaps there was no sense in wasting more energy on him. Turning abruptly to Sally, he stared at her.

"Well?" he asked, half afraid of asking the question for fear of what her answer might be. "Are you coming with me, or staying here with him and his jo-fired gold?"

She didn't answer for a moment, first staring at him with troubled blue eyes and then glancing over at Seamus, who kept his gaze trained on his boots as he pulled them on. Then she let out a quick little sigh and nodded.

"I'll come with you," she told James softly. "I think you're right; it might be best if I were to stay out of sight for a while. Just in case."

Relief flooded through James. Until that moment, he hadn't quite realized how important it was that Sally come with him to Sonoma. He glanced over at Seamus, almost ashamed of such feelings. Seamus looked suddenly very small and helpless sitting there, crouched over his boots with his head down.

For a moment James almost changed his mind. What harm would it do to stay and prospect for a few weeks? They could always go to Sonoma after that; as Seamus had mentioned, it would make it easier to hire horses if they had a bit more money to their names.

Sally turned to Seamus, who was still fiddling with his boots. "Won't you change your mind, Seamus?" she asked. "Please come with us."

"No thank you," Seamus said, his tone and expression mulish. "I came here for gold, not to be bossed around by another member of the Gates family. It was bad enough when it was Arthur; at least he provided a proper roof over my head." He kicked out at the post of his tent.

Anger bubbled up in James and erupted before he could stop it. "Oh, yes?" he snapped. "And here I thought you'd come west chasing your ridiculous conspiracies. Missing anti-Masons, wasn't it? In any case, your father didn't seem to mind following mine back in their youth. From what you say, he even got some financial benefit out of it—not to mention a home and family, which he lacked before."

Seamus jumped to his feet. "Don't you dare talk about my father that way!" he shouted. "He made his own way in this world, and I intend to do the same."

Without waiting for a response, Seamus stomped off and disappeared into the bushes. Sally called after him anxiously, but there was no response.

"Aren't you going to do something?" she pleaded, turning to James. "You can't allow him to rush off in anger like that."

"Oh, really?" James muttered. "In fact, I think that I *can* allow it."

His stomach twisted with guilt, but he ignored it. Seamus's mention of Arthur had only strengthened his resolve. He had not come all this way only to allow another to make decisions for him. Not Arthur, not his father, not Seamus, not anyone.

"I'll be back soon," he told Sally. "I want to find Grizzly and see if he can advise us on the best way to get some horses."

Grizzly Adams wound up not only finding them a pair of sturdy mules for the journey, but also guiding them part of the way himself. He left them after a couple of days with good directions and a crude hand-drawn map—which, together with good weather, allowed James and Sally to make excellent time in reaching Sonoma. Once they were safely away from Hangtown, Sally had traded in her boy's clothes for a woman's riding habit she had purchased in Missouri.

"I know it is a greater risk," she had said when James expressed surprise and concern. "But disguising myself has become tiresome, and I must break away from the practice if I am ever to feel fully free."

James accepted that without further argument. He still worried that she might be more easily recognized if indeed her father was looking for her here. However, after traveling for so long now with no sign of further pursuit, it seemed a bit easier to relax—to assume that, despite Sally's fears about her father, he had indeed given up on finding her. Besides that, James had to admit he found pleasure in seeing Sally in female clothes again.

They arrived in the bustling town of Sonoma in the early afternoon of a sunny, pleasant day. The place was laid out around an eight-acre central plaza that offered agreeable views of the mountains to the north from nearly every angle. This plaza was bordered by a road populated by numerous carriages, riders, and pedestrians. James soon spotted the mission Mr. Charbonneau had mentioned, which consisted of a small adobe church, several older, ramshackle wooden buildings, and an overgrown orchard, vineyard, and garden. Across the street from the mission, on the northeast corner of the plaza, were newly constructed adobe barracks. Other buildings and houses surrounded the plaza, but the newcomers were quickly pointed to the Sonoma House, also referred to by a few people as the Blue Wing Inn. This was a large adobe hotel and general store near the mission, where James and Sally found many locals willing to answer all their questions about the area.

"Three hills, eh?" an old man with a pipe said when asked. "Doesn't narrow things down much. Lots of hills in these parts."

Mr. Cooper, a retired sailor who was coproprietor of the place, stopped mopping the store's counter with a rag. "Not so fast, Silas," he said. "Three hills between sea and creek? Sounds like the area down southwest of town to me. You can see the sea from there in some places."

Another man nodded. "Aye, there's a spot just a few miles out of town where you got a view of hills, sea, and creek all at once," he offered. "That sound like what you're lookin' for?"

"It does," James said eagerly. "Thank you! Could you kindly point us in that direction?"

Soon he and Sally were back on their mules, making their way along a dirt road leading to the spot the man had mentioned. "Do you really suppose this is it?" Sally asked, pulling at the reins to prevent her mule from dipping its head in pursuit of some green grass beside the road. "The end of this rather confusing, yet oddly diverting, quest?"

"We shall soon find out." Despite his neutral words, James found his heart beating faster with anticipation. Could this be it? Were they about to discover whatever it was that Aunt Ellie had left or discovered for them?

If it is indeed a vein of gold, Seamus shall regret not coming with us, he thought, though his anger had cooled in the days since his argument with Seamus.

"I wonder if we should have brought some digging tools," he mused aloud. "It seems unlikely that any gold or treasure or other valuables should be left out in plain view on a public road. We shall likely have to dig or something."

"We can always return to town for the necessary equipment. It is perhaps too late in the day to begin such an endeavor anyway." Sally shaded her eyes against the sun, which was just beginning to sink toward the western horizon. "Look—could that be it just ahead?"

James glanced forward. The road had just crested a steep hill, and now the sun's golden-orange rays illuminated a trio of smaller hills rising one after the other directly ahead. The only visible sign of civilization aside from the road itself was a comfortable-looking homestead consisting of a log house, a small barn, and a few chickens pecking in the yard. Glancing to the right, James caught a glimpse of the shimmering expanse of the ocean off in the distance. At left, just beyond the log house, a silvery creek tumbled busily over its bed of stone and lichen.

"This must be the spot," James said. "This is where we should find what we are seeking—whatever that may be!"

Sally glanced around. "But where exactly?" she asked as she slid down from the saddle. "There seems to be nothing to direct us more specifically either in clue or landscape. And I expect the owners of that house should not be pleased if we were to start digging up the road or their land."

At that moment the door of the house opened. A silver-haired woman stood there peering out at them. She appeared to be in her sixties and was dressed in a modest housedress with a homespun apron tied over it.

"Can I help you, strangers?" she called out.

James felt a flash of impatience. He had come to find his fortune, not to make small talk with old ladies. But Sally's last comment made him realize that it might be prudent to stay on the good side of the homesteaders that owned this property.

"Good afternoon, ma'am," he said politely, leaving the mules ground-tied and walking toward the woman with Sally beside him. "We're exceedingly sorry to intrude. This is Miss Sally Chandler, and my name is James Madison Gates. We were looking for a spot that matches this description, and—"

The old woman cut off his words with a gasp so mighty that for a second James feared she was succumbing to old age right before their eyes. He was equally startled when she rushed forward and clasped both his hands in her own.

"Oh, sakes alive!" the woman exclaimed, her wrinkled old face bursting into a brilliant smile even as tears poured from her faded blue eyes. "I can hardly believe it can be true! But of course it is—you are the very image of your father at that age, though of course his hair was a bit darker." She laughed at his look of confusion. "James, it is I—your Aunt Ellie!"

Nineteen

James was stunned. Aunt Ellie? Before he quite managed to gather his wits about him, he found himself following Sally through the log house's front door into a small but cheerful room brightened by colorful rag rugs and a pretty quilt hanging on one wall. Fortunately, Sally had not been rendered quite so speechless as James by this turn of events, and by the time they were all seated on wooden chairs around a low table decorated with a pot of wildflowers, she had begun to extract the full story from Aunt Ellie.

"It was all meant as a sort of game," the old woman explained as she poured them some tea. "Similar to the puzzles and codes that we amused ourselves with when we were young, which I'd missed dearly since coming west—nearly as dearly as I missed Adam himself." She sighed and gazed at James. "It is so good to see your face, dear boy, and his in yours. But please—how is your father lately? Is he well?"

"He—he is well, I suppose," James stammered, still trying to wrap his head around everything. "At least he was when I left home close to a year ago now. But are you telling us there is no—no treasure at the end of the line? Did you never intend him to follow your clues? Or were they even meant as clues at all?"

Ellie smiled, a wistful look coming into her eyes. "Oh, I hoped that he would indeed follow them," she said. "It was really just my own clever little way of begging him to come west for a visit. You see, the treasure I had in mind was myself. Or rather, the reunion between the two of us after so many years."

"Oh!" Sally smiled. "I see it now. That's the meaning of 'dearest Treasure' from the first letter—we took it to mean 'dear' in the sense of expensive or such, but you meant it in the more personal sort of way. And I always thought it a bit odd that the last clue referenced 'the Treasure *whom* you seek' rather than 'the Treasure *that* you seek.' It is so obvious now that I think of it!"

Indeed, James could see it now as well. It *should* have been obvious, at least to one not blinded by dreams of wealth and respect. . . .

"Yes, I suppose it was rather indulgent for me to expect my dear brother to come all this way to see me," Aunt Ellie went on. "But I have been a bit lonely since my husband died."

"Oh, I am sorry!" Sally said. "My condolences, Mrs. Darby."

Ellie smiled at her. "Thank you, my dear," she said. "But you need not feel too sorry for me. I have had a long and full life, and have lived out most of my dreams, which mostly dealt with exploration and learning." She glanced toward some framed daguerreotypes hanging on the wall. "Besides that, my children live nearby, so I am not really alone. Still, I have often found myself thinking of home and old times these past few years. And Adam was always impulsive and ready for adventure, so I hoped he might be tempted."

"This explains why the clues merely continued pointing us west along the usual route," James said numbly. "Of course Father would have realized right away what you intended, so each new letter was merely further urging rather than a necessary step in continuing."

Ellie bowed her head in affirmation. "But that reminds me, James, how did you come to be following my letters without such information from your father? I must confess, when I realized it was you who came to me without him, well . . . I suppose I feared the worst."

James felt his cheeks go red. "Er, no, nothing like that," he mumbled. "Father doesn't exactly know that I have them. At least, he was not aware of it at the time I left. That is—"

To his surprise, Ellie started laughing. "Oh, I see," she exclaimed merrily, setting down her teacup and clapping her hands. "You absconded with them and took off on this adventure all without his knowledge! Ah, they say the apple does not fall far from the tree, and it seems that is true in this case."

This pronouncement startled James more than anything else so far on that surprising day. "Oh, no," he corrected hastily. "I'm afraid you are mistaken in thinking I am similar to Father. He and I may have the same nose and eyes and chin, but aside from that we have little in common."

"Do not be so sure," Aunt Ellie said, picking up her tea again and leaning back against the cushion on her chair with a knowing smile. "Who but a Gates man would pick up and head all the way across the continent due to a handful of cryptic clues?"

If Seamus had said such a thing, or even Sally, James might have protested or taken offense. Somehow, though, coming from Aunt Ellie it didn't sound quite so bad.

"In any case," Aunt Ellie went on, "I hope you're not too disappointed to have found no real treasure here, James."

"N-no, of course not," James stammered.

Naturally, this was not entirely true. He couldn't help being a bit disappointed to have his dreams of wealth dashed, even though he'd known all along that the likelihood of finding his fortune by following those clues was rather slim.

Oh, well, he thought, sipping from his teacup to hide his consternation. *I suppose now I really do have something in common with Father and the rest of the Gates men who have spent their lives searching for things that probably weren't there—and usually getting mocked for it.*

"I hope *you* are not disappointed, Aunt Ellie," he said after a moment. "I'm sorry that Father did not come himself. He is very busy with, er—has he told you of a certain clue my brother Thomas received from Charles Carroll?"

"*The secret lies with Charlotte,*" Ellie responded with a nod.

"Yes, he has written me of that often. I think he hopes I will be able to help him decipher it, as I often did with such things when we were young." She shrugged. "I have had no such luck. But I'm certain he shall crack it eventually, or perhaps your older brother Thomas—he seems quite clever from what I understand."

"Yes," James said. "He is."

She leaned forward and took his hand. "In any case, I am certainly not disappointed in the least to meet you at last, James," she said. "Your father has written of you often."

"He has?" James found himself stunned anew at that.

"Of course. He always writes how clever you are and how you are the most reliable and even-tempered member of the family. He's very proud of you, you know." If Aunt Ellie noticed his growing expression of shock, she did not let on. "I only wish your dear mother could have lived long enough to know you. I know she was terribly pleased when she discovered she was expecting you—just a month before you were born, she wrote to me that she anticipated great things from you."

"You knew my mother?" James's stomach twisted into

a painful little knot. Somehow, even though he'd known that Ellie hadn't moved to California until after he was born, he hadn't quite put those two facts together.

Ellie nodded. "Oh, but that reminds me . . ." Without further explanation, she stood up and hurried through a doorway into the next room.

"Man alive," Sally whispered as soon as she was out of view. "This is a most surprising end to our quest, is it not? But you must be so pleased to meet your aunt at last."

"Yes," James said, realizing it was true. Perhaps he had found a treasure after all, even if it was not the kind he was expecting.

Ellie returned after a moment, clutching something in her wrinkled hand. "Here you go, James," she said, handing it to him. "Your mother gave me this as a memento when she left Massachusetts. I know she would have wished you to have it now."

James looked down. In his hand was a small gold ring with his mother's initials carved into it.

"Thank you," he said, feeling a tightness in his throat as he gazed down at it. It seemed he had discovered gold in California after all, and not only of the monetary variety.

"Thank you. Er—perhaps you could tell me—tell me more about her?"

"Of course," Ellie replied. "I will gladly tell you everything you want to know."

The next two days seemed to speed by. Once his initial shock wore off, James enjoyed getting to know his aunt, as well as his cousins, who hurried to visit once news of his arrival reached them. Sally got on just as well as he did with Ellie, if not even better, and spent many hours debating and discussing with her the role of women in society, the likelihood that the abolitionists would succeed in their goals, the ways that President Taylor was confounding the Whigs who had nominated him, and various other political matters.

Still, by the second evening it was clear that Sally was growing restless. "I cannot help but think of poor Seamus, all alone back in that rough mining town," she explained as she and James headed outside into the twilight to tend to the mules.

"He isn't really alone," James pointed out. "I'm sure Grizzly will look after him, and perhaps Pomp Charbonneau as well."

"Yes, but that isn't the same as having us there," she insisted. "I think we ought to go back and check on him."

James busied himself with the animals' water trough to avoid having to answer right away. He had to admit he, too, had entertained a passing thought or two about how Seamus was doing. But that didn't mean he liked having Sally showing so much concern over him. When she'd chosen to accompany James on this last stage of their journey, he had taken that as meaning she preferred his company to that of Seamus. But was that entirely true, or was it only his own wishful interpretation of her decision?

In any event, it soon became clear that she would not rest until they returned to check on Seamus. And so, after promising Aunt Ellie that he would return as soon as he could, James and Sally prepared to make their return ride the next day.

James and Sally arrived back in Hangtown around noon on a warm but breezy day. They went first to the spot along the creek where they had all been panning before their departure. However, there was no sign of Seamus there, nor at their makeshift camp either, and so they headed into town to see if he might be there. The streets were nearly deserted, as most of the men were out prospecting. But on their way to the saloon, they passed Grizzly Adams and several other men coming from the outskirts of town with dirt on their hands and clothes. There was no sign of Ben around, and Grizzly's face was uncharacteristically solemn, at first leading James to wonder if something had happened to the bear.

"We have just buried the Reverend," Grizzly reported with sadness in his eyes. "He succumbed to cholera just this morning."

Sally gasped. "You don't mean Reverend James?" she cried, her hands flying to her mouth in horror.

"Aye, 'fraid I do," Grizzly said with a deep sigh. "Though I knew 'im only these few weeks, I could see he were a fine man and shall be missed."

James was shocked by the news. His thoughts flew immediately to the minister's brave young wife, even now awaiting his return back in Missouri, and to his young sons, Frank and Jesse, and the new baby, who would now grow up without a father just as James Gates himself had grown up without a mother.

In addition, he felt a sudden flare of concern for Seamus. He asked Grizzly if he'd seen him that day. "We already checked our strike and our tents, and he was not in either place," he explained.

"Ain't seen him today, no." Grizzly scratched his beard. "But he gave up on that panning spot three days ago. Just found a new place half a mile or so to the northeast."

"Will you show us, please?" Sally asked with such urgency that James suspected she was entertaining similar thoughts to his own.

"Promised to help these fellas find some wood to make a cross for the grave," Grizzly said with an apologetic shrug. "I can take you in an hour or so, though."

James knew that the proper thing to do would be to offer to help with the grave marker while awaiting Grizzly's guidance. But now that the seed of worry had been planted in his mind, he couldn't stand to wait any longer to locate his friend. All along he had blamed Sally's concern on either female weakness or overly warm feelings toward Seamus. But perhaps she had been right to insist on returning to check on him. If a strong, healthy man like Reverend James could succumb so quickly to cholera, who knew what dangers lurked for one such as Seamus, who had never been the most practical of fellows?

"Can you just tell us where to go, then?" he said. "I'm sure we can find the spot on our own."

Grizzly nodded agreeably and quickly described the spot and the easiest path to find it. "If you don't find him, let me know," he said. "I'll track 'im down for you."

The spot where Grizzly had sent them was higher up in the hills than the earlier one. He had described the new strike spot accurately as a smallish clearing with a cold, fast-running creek tumbling through it on its way downhill from the higher peaks. At the far side of the clearing the creek abruptly disappeared, splashing over the edge of a steep cliff into a narrow, rocky ravine some hundred feet deep. James and Sally had approached this spot along a narrow, twisting path through the thick woods along one edge of the ravine and so had no view of the clearing until they were at its edge. As soon as they emerged from the tangle of trees, however, they immediately spotted Seamus's familiar skinny figure leaning over the edge of the creek just a few yards ahead in the middle of the clearing.

"Seamus!" Sally cried with relief as soon as she spotted him.

Seamus turned immediately. His face was glowing, and he let out a happy shout.

"I've done it!" he cried, rushing toward them. "You got here just in time—I found gold! The creek is brimming with it! We're going to be rich!"

He was practically bubbling over with excitement, and James guessed that he was too thrilled with his discovery to remember that he'd been angry with them when they left. For James's part, he felt his heart flip over. Could it be true? Had they truly struck it rich, just as they had hoped and imagined?

"Well, what are we waiting for?" he exclaimed with a grin, clapping Seamus on the back. "Let's get it out of there!"

They spent the next half hour or so panning furiously. Seamus's enthusiasm had not been misplaced; good-size nuggets shone out from among the river stones at every scoop.

"This is extraordinary!" Sally sat back on her heels, pushing her hair out of her face, which was glowing pink with delight. "There is enough here to keep us all living well for at least a year."

Seamus nodded. "I want to give Grizzly a cut," he said. "He was the one who told me of this spot. I understand it's a favorite napping place for Ben during hot weather."

Sally laughed. "Then I suppose we ought to give Ben a cut as well."

"That sounds fair enough." James laughed along, still hardly daring to believe their good fortune. After a lifetime of disappointment and dullness, it was almost overwhelming. "There's plenty for all of us here!"

"Not so fast," a man's deep voice growled. "I'll take that gold, if you please. And Miss Chandler, too."

James jumped, so startled he nearly fell into the creek. Spinning around, he gasped in horror. Mr. Chandler's swarthy, oversize henchman from Baltimore was standing at the edge of the woods. And he was holding Aunt Ellie in front of him, a gleaming silver knife at her throat!

Twenty

"**A**unt Ellie!" James cried.

"Who?" Seamus said. "Huh?" He blinked. "Hey! You're that fellow. . . ." His words trailed off and he gulped, clearly realizing that this was bad news.

James took a step toward the man. The thug must have been following them for some time—since Aunt Ellie's house at least. Perhaps he'd just been biding his time, waiting for the perfect chance to snatch Sally away. In any case, he'd clearly seen Aunt Ellie as the ideal hostage.

"Please." James choked on the words. "Let her go."

"I'm all right, James," Ellie called out. "Whatever this terrible man wants, don't give in!"

"Silence!" the man roared, giving Ellie a little jab with the tip of the knife.

"No!" Sally cried. "Please. It's all right—I'll come with you quietly. Just let Mrs. Darby go."

The man smirked. "Tell you what, Miss Chandler," he

growled. "Why don't you pick up that nice, shiny gold and bring it over here, along with your pretty little outlaw self. Then we'll see about letting the old lady go."

"Sally . . ." James began in a strangled tone.

She ignored him, scooping up handfuls of the gold they'd just panned. "It's all right," she said, her face now as white and strained as it had been pink and joyful a few moments earlier. "I knew it was too good to last. I'll go with him, and you all will be safe." She turned her sad eyes to Seamus, then James. "I'm sorry about the gold. But you two can find more—I know you can." She swallowed a sob. "You'll do fine."

"Listen to her, boys," the thug said. "Whatever gold you find once I leave is yours, but this here's mine. And a nice bonus it'll make to the reward waitin' for me back in Baltimore." He chuckled. "Told those fools the trip out here would be worthwhile, seasickness, scurvy, and all. And them still huntin' around like fools back in Missouri. . . ."

James suspected that these last gloating comments were not really meant for them. But he wasn't really paying attention to what the man was saying, anyway. He couldn't let this happen! He couldn't allow this man to hustle Sally off back to Baltimore and the life she dreaded. However, he knew her well enough by now to know that she would never forgive herself if Aunt Ellie were hurt or killed because of her. So he forced himself to wait, hoping the thug would be honorable enough to let his aunt go once he had his quarry. After that, perhaps James could do something. . . .

"That's better," the thug said when Sally reached him. In one swift movement, he grabbed her and shoved Aunt Ellie away. The older woman stumbled a little on the loose shale, teetering dangerously close to the edge of the ravine. Seamus was the closest; he leaped toward Aunt Ellie and caught her, easing her back to safety.

"Thank you, young man." Ellie peered at him. "You must be the Seamus Poole I've heard so much about. I'm James's Aunt Ellie."

"Quiet!" the thug barked out before Seamus could respond. "This ain't no quiltin' bee." He was hanging on to Sally with one meaty hand, scrabbling to stuff the gold nuggets into his clothes with the other. Most of the nuggets missed the mark and tumbled to the ground, causing the man to let out several colorful oaths.

He bent to retrieve the gold. When he did, both Sally

and James sprang into action simultaneously. Sally kicked out, catching the man in the shin with the sharp toe of her shoes. Meanwhile James ran straight at him with a yell, not having any particular plan in mind and knowing that the man was nearly double his size and weight.

But it didn't matter. James had to rescue Sally or die trying. After all, what point was there in going on without her, knowing she was living in misery back in Baltimore? He wouldn't be able to stand it.

"Hey!" the man shouted. Abandoning the fallen gold for the moment, he straightened up and sent Sally reeling with a backhand to the side of her face. James was almost upon him when he reached around and pulled a revolver out of the back of his pants, pointing it straight at James's face.

"Stop right there, boy!" he roared out.

James skidded to a stop, staring into the muzzle of the gun. His thoughts were frozen by the weapon's sudden appearance.

"Back up. Over there with your friends," the thug ordered coldly, gesturing with the gun to where Seamus was still standing with Aunt Ellie. "You know, I was gonna be a nice guy and let you all go about your business. You've just convinced me that that would be a mistake." He raised the gun and sighted down it, aiming straight at Seamus.

"No!" Sally cried from the ground, where she was crouched, her hand to her face. "Please don't!"

James's head spun. He had just made everything even worse. True, he had been more than willing to die for Sally. But he hadn't expected to doom Seamus and Aunt Ellie as well. . . .

ROAAAARRRRRR!

The sudden, spine-tingling bellow echoed off the trees and bounced back at them from the ravine, seeming to grow even louder. Seconds later an enormous grizzly bear charged into the clearing, teeth bared and hackles raised.

James gasped. It was Ben—or was it? This beast looked nothing like the docile creature he normally saw shambling along behind Grizzly Adams.

The thug let out a surprisingly high-pitched scream. He whirled around and pointed his gun at the bear. But his hand was shaking, and the shot went wide, bouncing harmlessly off a rock. A second later Ben—if it was indeed Ben—leaped at him, knocking him to the ground and sending the gun flying out of his hand and over the edge of the ravine.

"No!" the man shrieked, rolling out of the way of the bear's swiping paw and clambering to his feet. "Noooooo!"

A whistle came from the direction of the woods. The bear glanced over his shoulder and then sat down on its haunches and started licking his paw like an enormous cat.

James breathed out a sigh of relief. "It *is* Ben!" he called to the others.

Sally and Seamus looked relieved, too, though Aunt Ellie appeared rather confused. The thug continued to look terrified, especially when Ben finished washing his paw and stood up.

"Stay back!" the man howled as Ben ambled forward a few steps.

At that moment Grizzly Adams and Pomp Charbonneau appeared at the edge of the woods. Grizzly's eyes widened as he took in the situation.

"Stand still!" he called to the thug. "He ain't gonna hurt you."

The thug didn't seem to hear him, or even note his presence. His small, round eyes remained fixed on the bear.

"You won't get me, creature of the devil!" he yelled, backing up as Ben took another step toward him, sniffing curiously.

"Wait," Seamus called. "You're too close to the . . ."

"*AAAAAAAAAAAH!*" The man had just taken another step backward—this time into nothingness. His left foot plunged over the edge of the ravine. He tried to lurch forward and catch himself, but his own bulk was working against him. With one last piercing scream, he disappeared from sight. Seconds later there came a soft thud from somewhere far below.

Grizzly winced, then shrugged. "Tried to warn 'im," he muttered. Glancing at James, he added with concern, "Friend of yours?"

"Not exactly." James stepped forward to peer over the edge of the cliff. He flinched at what he saw at the bottom, and turned quickly to prevent Sally from following suit.

"Don't look," he advised her. "I'm afraid it's too late for him."

"Good riddance," Grizzly muttered darkly. "Figured that one was up to no good, eh, Pompy?"

Pomp Charbonneau nodded. "I spotted him on my way into town," he explained. He nodded toward Aunt Ellie.

245

"When I saw him dragging this lady along with him, seemed right suspicious. So I thought I'd better follow along and see what was up. . . ."

". . . and when Ben and I encountered him along the way, I figured I'd stick my big old nose into it as well," Grizzly finished with a chuckle. "Guess it's a good thing we did."

"Indeed." James turned and smiled at Sally. He hardly dared to believe it was all over—perhaps for good this time. "It's a very good thing."

"Ah, there you are, my friend." James looked up and smiled as Seamus entered the Sonoma tavern and hurried toward the table where he was seated. "Torn yourself away from your saucy merchant's daughter long enough for a midday meal, eh?"

Seamus grinned and flopped into his seat. "Aye," he said. "But it is true, she keeps me busy. Not that I am complaining, mind you!"

James chuckled. Several months had passed since their adventures in Hangtown, and much had changed in that time—mostly for the better. He, Seamus, and Sally had ended up splitting the gold they'd found—what was left of it after the rest had plunged over the cliff with Mr. Chandler's thug, that is—with Grizzly Adams and Pomp Charbonneau. This had left them each with a modest fortune, perhaps less than their headier dreams had hoped for, but still more than enough to create a comfortable life for themselves in California.

And indeed, all of them had decided to stay. Seamus had pointed out that there was still nothing for him back in the States, though he traded letters regularly with his sister. James suspected that a large part of his friend's decision to stay was the dark-haired, rosy-cheeked beauty he'd met soon after finding that gold. She was bright, intelligent, almost as interested in women's suffrage as Sally . . . and talked nearly as much as Seamus did himself!

As for James, there had been no question about what he would do. Sally had escaped her father's clutches, seemingly for good, but she would never be able to return to the East. And wherever Sally chose to make her home, that would be James's home as well. Coming so close to losing her this last time had helped him realize once and for all that he was in love with her. Fortunately, she returned his feelings fully, and with Aunt Ellie's blessing, James had given her his mother's gold ring. They had married as soon as they could find a minister to perform the ceremony. Afterward, James had written to his father to share the news—and to send a portion of his gold to pay him back for the coach and horses he'd lost in Missouri. This had started a correspondence between father and son that had started to heal the rift that had always existed between them. James found it rather ironic that it was only with the breadth of an entire continent lying between them that they had finally grown a bit closer.

"Had any news from back home lately?" Seamus inquired as the tavern owner's daughter brought him a plate of meat and he tucked in.

James nodded. "I had a letter from Eleanor this week," he said. "She reports that Father remains in good health for his age. In fact, he and Thomas have just returned from yet another trip to the city of Charlotte, North Carolina."

"Another?" James laughed. "I fear those two shall never give up on finding the mysterious Charlotte and her even more mysterious secret!"

James smiled along, but for just a moment he felt a pang of regret for lost opportunities. Would his father and

Thomas indeed ever solve the mystery of "Charlotte"? Should he have tried harder to get involved with their interests when he was at home? Might that have changed things? With the distance between them now, he found himself more often smiling than frowning at his memories of them—of roughhousing with Thomas when they were much younger, or watching with admiration as his father skillfully trained a young horse to harness . . .

"Never mind," he said, shaking his head to clear it of all melancholy thoughts and pointless nostalgia. He might have done better at times, it was true. But in the end, he had no real regrets about how his life had turned out. "They are no worse than you, after all," he teased Seamus playfully. "Just consider your quests for conspiracies and uncovering the secrets of the Freemasons and such. Is that any better than Charlotte in the end?"

Seamus grinned. "Perhaps when I'm your father's age, I'll be able to return to such pursuits," he said. "For now, between my Mary and the business, I am far too busy."

That was true enough, as James well knew. For the first month or so after striking gold, the friends had continued to search for more. But when they had come up mostly empty-handed, James had convinced Seamus to pool his remaining fortune so that the two of them could open up a store in Sonoma catering to forty-niners and newcomers to the area. Aunt Ellie helped run the place now, as did Sally, Seamus's Mary, and several of James's cousins and second cousins. It was already quite successful; so much so that James no longer worried over whether Sally might start to miss her luxurious lifestyle from back east.

The two friends finished their meal and then stood to go. As they left the tavern, squinting in the bright California sunshine, a slender, bespectacled man stopped them. He was older than Aunt Ellie, perhaps in his mid-seventies, and had only a tuft of white hair around his otherwise bald pate.

"Pardon me," he said, pausing before them. "My name is Gordon; I am a stranger in these parts newly arrived from the Spanish south."

"Spanish, eh?" Seamus said with a smile. "By your accent, I'll wager you were not born amongst the Mexicans however."

The man chuckled. "Indeed you are correct, sir," he admitted. "I come originally from Virginia, though I have lived in Canada, New York, and well nigh everywhere else on this great continent over the course of my life."

"New York, eh?" Seamus said. "I was born in that great state myself."

"Indeed? Well, it is a fine thing to meet a neighbor so far from home." The man nodded his head pleasantly. "In any case, might you gentlemen be able to tell me where I could purchase a healthy mule? My horse has gone lame, and I have a goodly distance still to go before I rest."

"There is a livery just there where you might have some luck," Seamus replied, pointing to the establishment in question, which was across the street. "Out of curiosity, how far are you going? It is late in the season if you are heading all the way back to the States."

"Oh, I shall not be traveling quite so far," the man said with a smile. "I have heard that Brigham Young and many of his Mormon followers have settled in the Salt Lake Valley, and have interest in seeing it for myself."

His mention of the Mormons reminded James of the incident with the Mormon boy during their journey out, and he smiled to himself. Sally often said it was that moment that she'd fallen in love with him. . . .

251

He was so distracted by such thoughts that he almost missed Seamus's next question: "What did you say your name was, sir?" Seamus asked. "And where exactly in New York did you live, if you don't mind my asking?"

"Gordon. My name is Will Gordon," the man replied with a tip of his hat. "Thank you kindly for your advice. Now I'm afraid I must go."

"Wait!" Seamus blurted out as the man scurried off. But it was too late. He had already disappeared around the corner.

"What's the matter?" James asked.

Seamus turned to stare at him, wide-eyed. "Gordon," he said slowly. "Mr. Will Gordon. Doesn't that name sound remarkably like . . . Mr. William Morgan?"

"Don't be foolish," James said automatically. "That couldn't possibly be your mysterious missing Mr. Morgan." He paused, glancing in the direction the man had gone. "Could it?"

"Come on. Let's see if we can catch him." Seamus hurried off down the block with James at his heels.

But no matter how they searched, they could not find hide nor hair of Mr. Gordon again, and no one else they asked seemed to have made his acquaintance. They finally gave up, wandering back toward their store in the pleasantly rosy glow of the setting sun.

"Do you really think it could have been him?" Seamus asked wistfully, glancing over his shoulder as if hoping the mysterious man would appear even now.

James shrugged. "I suppose we'll never know," he said with a smile, reaching over to clap his friend on the back. "Much like whatever secret lies with Charlotte, perhaps some mysteries are meant to remain unsolved."

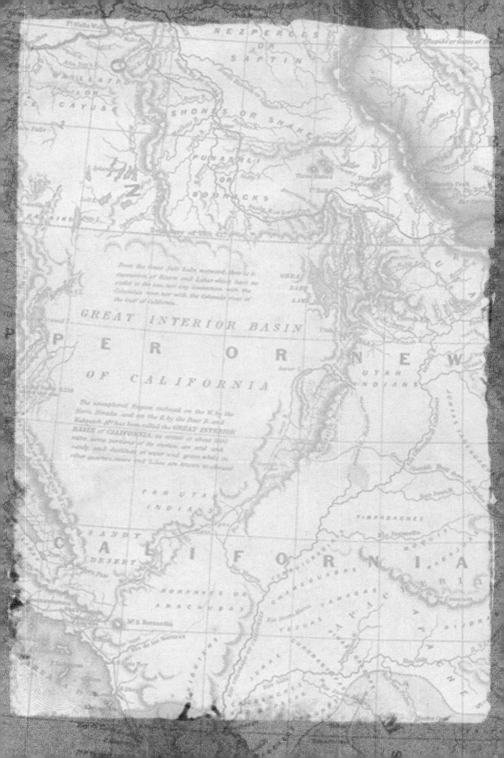

Post Script

Like the films *National Treasure* and *National Treasure: Book of Secrets* that inspired it, this book is a fictional story grounded in real facts and history. James Madison Gates, his family, Seamus Poole, Sally Chandler, and some of the other characters are invented. But many others who appear in the story were real people who lived at that time, and many of the events that James witnesses, hears about, or discusses actually did take place.

For instance, there really was a celebration to mark the placing of the cornerstone of the Washington Monument on July 4, 1848. It was sponsored by the Freemasons, of which Washington and then-President Polk were members, and most other details mentioned about the event are based on fact.

Speaking of the Freemasons, when Seamus discusses becoming a "third-degree Freemason" with Meriwether Clark, it reveals the origin of the common phrase "to give someone the third degree." This is based on the requirements for reaching the status of Master Mason, or third degree of Masonry.

William Morgan was a real person, who really did disappear under mysterious circumstances in 1826, probably due to his anti-Mason activities as mentioned in the story. It is speculated by some that his wife became one of the plural wives of Mormon founder Joseph Smith, Jr. (Morgan's own fate has never been determined. Therefore his possible appearance in California is, of course, fictional!)

And speaking of Joseph Smith, Jr., the Mormon history mentioned here is all based on fact. The group was persecuted before and after the death of their leader in 1844, and many travelers made their way from the city of Nauvoo west along the Mormon Trail—which ran parallel to the Oregon Trail—to settle in Utah and elsewhere. (Also, Joseph Smith himself really was a treasure hunter in his younger days!)

As for the Oregon Trail, most of the landmarks mentioned here are real, including Courthouse Rock, Chimney Rock, Ash Hollow, and the Platte, Snake, and Raft Rivers. (By the way, once travelers had reached any of those landmarks, they would have considered themselves well outside of "the States," which is how Americans in those days referred to the settled areas east of the Mississippi River area.)

Many other physical landmarks mentioned in the story, including the National Road; Grinder's Stand (where Meriwether Lewis died); Hannibal, Missouri; Hangtown (now known as Placerville, California); and Sonoma, California, (including the Blue Wing Inn, which remains there to this day), are real as well. The three hills spot and Ellie's house are, however, quite fictional.

Several of the people James and his friends meet were real-life figures, too.

Robert James (father of famous outlaw Jesse James) was a minister who really did travel west with a wagon train and died soon after arriving in Hangtown (though the year of his journey has been adjusted by a year to fit with the rest of the story).

Samuel Clemens grew up to become Mark Twain, the famous author. He lived in Hannibal, Missouri, worked as a printer's apprentice after his father's death, and later went to work for his brother, Orion, a newspaperman. (The brothers' acquaintance with Robert James is fictional.)

Clark's son, Meriwether Clark, was also a real person, though his visit to Baltimore and other details are invented for this story. Grizzly Adams was real as well (with a real pet bear named Benjamin Franklin), as was Jean-Baptiste "Pomp" Charbonneau, who was born to his mother Sacagawea during the Lewis and Clark expedition. Both Adams and Charbonneau were involved in the California Gold Rush, though their friendship as portrayed here is fictional.

Other real-life figures mentioned include Charles Carroll of Carrollton; Queen Victoria of England; President John Quincy Adams; President Zachary Taylor and his opponents in the election of 1848; William L. Todd (nephew of First Lady Mary Todd Lincoln); Kit Carson; John C. Frémont; Moses Bates and Abraham Bird; Brigham Young; Nostradamus; and the Donner Party. (A group of settlers who became trapped in the Sierra Nevada when a snowstorm hit, they had to resort to cannibalism to stay alive.)

Lucretia Mott and Elizabeth Cady Stanton, mentioned in the story by Sally, were real-life abolitionists and champions of women's rights. They did attend the World Anti-Slavery Convention in London as mentioned, and also convened the Seneca Falls Convention. (It is unlikely that Sally could have planned ahead to attend the convention, which was announced just a few days before it took place!**)**

Other real-life events include the Mexican-American War, the Bear Flag Revolt and short-lived California Republic, the New Madrid Earthquake of 1812, and, of course, the California Gold Rush itself.

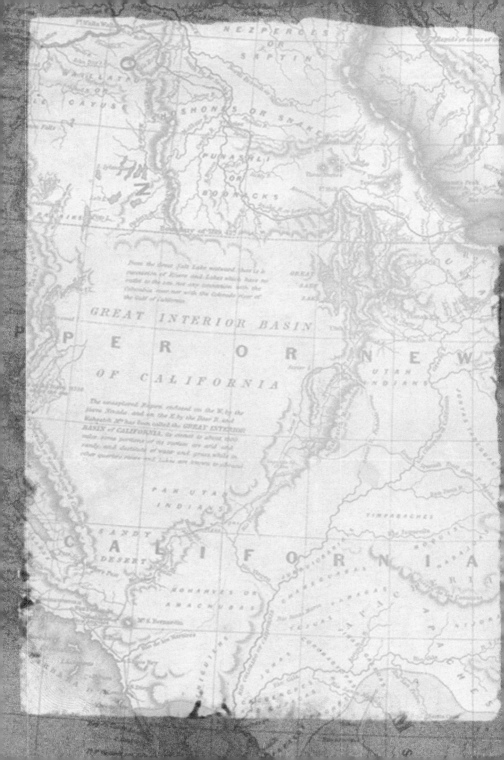

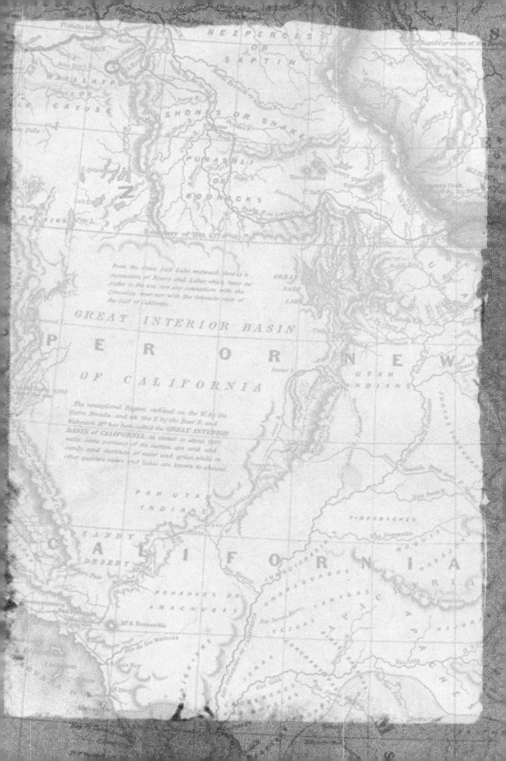

DON'T MISS THE NEXT VOLUME...

FOREVER FREE

⚓ A GATES *Family Mystery* ⚓

In the late 1800s, the North defeated the South in the Civil War, Abraham Lincoln signed the Emancipation Proclamation, and America found herself in the middle of the reconstruction era. This brought prosperity, joy, and equality to many of the freed slaves. But for others, the past is too haunting to forget.

Maryland. 1872. After the death of his father, Charles Gates wants nothing more than to turn his back on his family's never-ending quest for treasure. But then he meets Daniel, a young freed slave who needs his help. Now, along with Daniel, Charles sets off on a journey to uncover a treasure that civil rights figures like Frederick Douglass, Harriet Beecher Stowe, and Sojourner Truth fought to protect, never lose, and keep . . . forever free.

[9]